FANTAIL BOOKS

Super Mario Brothers

D1352238

Super Mario Brothers

A NOVEL BY
TODD STRASSER

BASED ON THE SCREENPLAY WRITTEN BY
PARKER BENNET & TERRY RUNTÉ
AND ED SOLOMON

FANTAIL

To Steven and Kelly Florio, Nintendo experts,
and to their parents, with great appreciation

FANTAIL BOOKS

Published by the Penguin Group
Penguin Books Ltd, 27 Wrights Lane, London w8 5tz, England
Penguin Books USA Inc., 375 Hudson Street, New York, 10014, USA
Penguin Books Australia Ltd, Ringwood, Victoria, Australia
Penguin Books Canada Ltd, 10 Alcorn Avenue, Toronto, Ontario, Canada m4v 3b2
Penguin Books (NZ) Ltd, 182–190 Wairau Road, Auckland 10, New Zealand

Penguin Books Ltd, Registered Offices: Harmondsworth, Middlesex, England

First published in the United States by Hyperion Books for Children 1993
First published in Great Britain by Fantail 1993
3 5 7 9 10 8 6 4 2

Fantail Film and TV Tie-in edition first published 1993

Text copyright © Hyperion Books for Children, 1993
Artwork logo copyright © Allied Filmmakers N.V. & Buena Vista
Pictures Distribution, Inc., 1993
Copyright © Nintendo, 1993
All rights reserved

Photography by Merie W. Wallace

Typeset by Datix International Limited, Bungay, Suffolk
Filmset in 13/15 pt Monophoto Baskerville
Printed in England by Clays Ltd, St Ives plc

I

Brooklyn, sixty-five million years ago

It was a time when the earth was young. Volcanoes spewed grey ash into the sky and spilled boiling red lava on to the ground. The oceans were warm, and the planet's surface was covered with marshes and lush green vegetation.

Many animals inhabited the seas and lands. But towering over all of them were the greatest creatures that ever roamed the earth – the mighty dinosaurs.

Day after day, huge meteorites pierced the sky and crashed on to the earth's surface. Most were simply cold, lifeless rocks. But one was different. It crashed into the earth with an explosion so great it hurled the dinosaurs into another dimension. There they continued to evolve into intelligent, voracious, highly aggressive beings ... just like humans.

2

Brooklyn, twenty years ago

*C*rack! Thunder crashed and lightning flashed in the stormy night sky. Heavy rain washed over the darkened streets. Clutching a bundle tightly in her arms, a beautiful young woman dressed in black ran down the street. Wet strands of her thick blonde hair fell into her large brown eyes, but she had no time to push them away as she splashed through the puddles.

She knew she was being followed. Somewhere in the dark, Koopa was searching for her. With his keen sense of smell, it wouldn't be long before he found her.

Ahead, a burst of lightning illuminated the tall, pointed spires of a church. The young woman stopped and stared. Was it a sign? Dare she go there? Could they ever understand? There was no time to waste; she had to take the chance.

She raced across the street and hurried up the church steps. Gently, she placed the bundle just outside the wooden doors. As tears mixed with the rain on her face, the young woman took out a small cone-shaped rock. She slipped it into a small slot inside the bundle, knocked twice on the wooden door, and then sprinted away into the rainy night.

She couldn't stop running. She had to lead Koopa away from what he wanted. As she dashed across the street, a horn blared, and a car skidded to avoid hitting her. The young woman jumped to get out of the way.

Thwack! She collided with a dark figure who'd just stepped from the shadows. Knocked to the ground, the stunned young woman swept the wet tangle of hair out of her eyes. She gasped in terror. Koopa!

With an evil smile, he bent down and offered her his hand. But the young woman jumped up and darted past him into a dark, cavernous subway entrance. Cursing, Koopa ran to follow.

Downstairs, the young woman raced along an empty subway platform, then jumped down on to the tracks. She could hear Koopa's loud footsteps behind her. Searching around her, she spotted an abandoned tunnel. The entrance was boarded up, but she quickly prised off a piece of plywood and squeezed inside.

The tunnel opened into a cavern supported bv

rotted timbers that looked as though they might give way at any moment. But it was too late to worry about that. Scrambling over the loose stones and dirt, the young woman quickly headed towards the other end of the tunnel. Ahead was an unusual-looking rock formation. She had to reach it before Koopa caught her!

Just then a hand grabbed her collar. The young woman cried out in pain as Koopa spun her around and pinned her roughly against the wall. His blond hair was slicked back. His skin had an unnatural sheen. His gaze was intense, almost hypnotic, and his face was strangely handsome.

'Where is the rock?' he asked, his controlled voice barely masking his fury.

The young woman pressed her lips firmly together and didn't answer. Koopa needed the meteorite piece to merge the dinosaur world with the mammal world. Then he would attack the mammals and eventually rule them, and everything she'd fought so hard for would be lost.

Looking around desperately, the young woman spied one of the rotten support beams holding up the tunnel ceiling. With one last burst of strength, she broke free of Koopa's grip and flung herself against it. It creaked and trembled, then splintered.

Crash! Koopa jumped back as a torrent of rocks

4

and dirt from the ancient ceiling tumbled around him, instantly crushing the young woman. Blast it! he thought. He looked back up the tunnel towards the subway tracks. Should he go back and try to find the meteorite piece? No; the gateway would close soon. There was no time left. Cursing with frustration, he turned and disappeared deeper into the cavern.

Back at the Brooklyn church, the wooden doors creaked open and two nuns peered out into the stormy night. They'd heard a knock, but there was no one outside.

'Look!' one whispered, pointing at the bundle on the steps.

'What is it?' asked the other.

'Let's see.' The first nun picked up the bundle and took it inside. She placed it on a table and carefully began to unwrap it, at last revealing a large egg-shaped metal container. Embedded in the container was the small cone-shaped rock. The second nun picked it up and looked at it curiously.

'I've never seen anything like it,' the first nun whispered.

'Look, a clasp,' said the other.

'Should we open it?'

'Yes.'

The first nun slowly opened the container, then gasped. Inside was a mottled dark-green egg.

'I've never seen an egg so big,' she whispered. 'It must be two feet long.'

Suddenly, the egg began to shake. The nuns quickly backed away and stared with wide eyes. A crack appeared in the eggshell. Then another. Something inside was trying to get out.

Finally the egg split open, and something small and pink poked out. One of the nuns screamed.

It was a tiny human hand.

3

Brooklyn, today

The street was lined with five-storey brick apartment blocks. Metal fire escapes criss-crossed their fronts. Women leaned on window-sills, watching children play in the street. Busy shoppers went in and out of bakers, launderettes, and newsagents.

Inside one of the buildings, in a small apartment, a short, solidly built man sat at a wooden desk, talking on the phone. He wore a light-blue work shirt and khaki trousers. His name was Mario Mario, and like his father, grandfather, and great-grandfather before him, he sported a thick black moustache.

Mario hung up the phone and jumped to his feet. 'Hey, Luigi!' he shouted to his brother. 'We got a broken dishwasher at the Bella Napoli restaurant.'

Luigi Mario was lying on the couch in the living-room, staring at the TV. He was wearing a white T-shirt, white jeans, and a white baseball cap backwards on his head. Luigi was taller and better-looking than Mario, and unlike his brother, he didn't wear a thick black moustache.

Pulling on a jacket, Mario hurried into the living-room. The furniture was old and a little shabby. Most of it had been purchased by Mario's great-grandfather and never replaced. But Mario liked that. He believed in tradition.

'Hey!' he yelled at Luigi. 'Did you hear me? We got work!'

'OK, but wait,' Luigi said, his eyes still glued to the TV. 'It's a special episode of *Our Miraculous World*: "Man Discovers He's an Alien!"'

Mario stuck his head between Luigi and the TV. 'The only miracle I know is that we're still eating when we're going broke.'

'Relax, Mario,' Luigi said. 'We ain't *going* broke. We're already there.'

'OK, OK,' Mario said impatiently. 'Now, let's go.'

While Luigi got ready, Mario quickly tidied up the living-room. Luigi was definitely the slob of the family. Mario took a Frisbee off the table and a hat off the lamp. Then he started piling up the crazy newspapers Luigi always bought. The one on top had stories about a baby with three arms and a kitten that performed miracles. Mario snorted.

'I can't believe you buy this rubbish,' he called into Luigi's room.

'Listen,' Luigi said, coming back into the living-room. 'That paper's got the article about the missing girls from Brooklyn – the ones that mysteriously disappeared without a trace. Some people think they were kidnapped by aliens.'

Mario stared at his brother. Sometimes it was hard to believe they came from the same parents. He glanced over at the fireplace, where a row of framed photographs lined the mantelpiece. There were pictures of his great-grandfather, his grandfather, and his father. All serious, hard-working plumbers with fine moustaches. It pained Mario that Luigi was so different. He doesn't even have a moustache! Mario thought sadly.

Moments later they were in their van. It was so old and badly dented that you could hardly see the lettering on the side, which read: Mario Brothers – Plumbers – Brooklyn's Best. Luigi drove, and Mario tried to find the restaurant on the map. But a loud scraping noise was distracting him.

'Hey!' he yelled to Luigi, who was swerving in and out of traffic. 'Is that noise from us?'

'Yeah!' Luigi called back. 'It's the exhaust pipe. We're dragging it.'

'Great!' Mario shouted. 'Another repair we

9

can't afford.' Suddenly he recognized a street sign. 'Hey, take a left here.'

The next thing he knew, Luigi took a hard screeching right and started speeding down an alleyway.

'What are you doing?' Mario gasped. 'I said left, not right.'

'Yeah, but I got a good feeling about this alley,' his brother said as he accelerated suddenly.

A second later the van skidded out of the alley-way and on to another street, narrowly missing several cars. Mario squeezed his eyes closed. Luigi quickly pulled over and stopped.

'What happened?' Mario gasped, holding his hand over his rapidly beating heart. 'Did we crash and go to heaven?'

'No, we went to the Bella Napoli,' Luigi said, pointing. 'What'd I tell you?'

Mario opened his eyes. 'It's a miracle we made it alive.'

'I thought you didn't believe in miracles,' Luigi said with a wink.

Mario groaned and turned towards the window. 'Oh no! Look!'

In the car-park of the restaurant was a new white van. Printed in big letters on the side was: Scapelli Construction, Plumbing, and Concrete.

'Not Scapelli!' Luigi groaned.

'We'd better get in there,' Mario said, pushing open his door.

The brothers hurried into the restaurant. They walked quickly across the dining-room and through the swinging doors to the kitchen, past bustling waiters and chefs in white uniforms. Finally they found a macho-looking man in a black tuxedo. Mario knew he was Pascal, the owner of the restaurant. Two big goons in Scapelli overalls were speaking to him.

'It's those slimeballs Doug and Mike,' Mario whispered to Luigi.

'Looks like a two-day job,' Doug was telling Pascal.

'Just to fix a dishwasher?' The restaurant owner scowled.

'If we can get the parts. It could be longer,' Mike added.

'Uh, excuse me,' Mario said, stepping between the Scapelli goons and Pascal. 'You said you had a dishwasher problem when you called *us* for the job.'

'Yes,' said Pascal, pointing at the dishwasher. 'It leaks from the bottom.'

Mario crouched down and looked at the dishwasher. A small puddle of water had collected on the floor beneath it. Mario stood up.

'You need a new gasket,' Mario said. 'Maybe a

hose. You're looking at a two-hour job. These Scapelli guys are trying to con you.'

'Would you excuse us, please?' Doug quickly grabbed Mario by his tool belt and yanked him over to a corner where Pascal couldn't hear.

'Hey!' Mario shouted, smacking Doug's hand away. 'Nobody touches my tools.'

The two Scapelli plumbers towered over him.

'Listen,' Mike hissed. 'I understand that nobody messes with your tools. And I assume you understand, Mario Mario, that nobody messes with us. Or our boss, Mr Scapelli. You know him?'

'Know him?' Mario had to laugh. 'I grew up with that bum. He ain't a plumber, he's a toxic-waste dumper. He don't know a pipe from a crow-bar.'

Doug and Mike glared at Mario, then turned back to the restaurant owner.

'I think Mr Scapelli will be pretty disappointed if he don't get this job,' Doug said.

'Yeah,' added Mike, staring hard at Pascal. 'So who you gonna hire? The Marios or Scapelli?'

Pascal swallowed. 'Uh, two days to fix a dishwasher sounds fine. I guess Scapelli gets the job.'

Mario's jaw dropped. Luigi's eyes bulged in disbelief. Pascal turned to them and whispered,

'I'll make it up to you, boys. How about a free dinner tonight?'

The Mario brothers sighed. A free meal was better than nothing.

4

Archaeological digs are an uncommon sight in Brooklyn, but on the day Luigi and Mario went to the Bella Napoli, a group of university students were sifting carefully through the rocks and dirt at a Scapelli building site near the bank of the East River.

Burly builders stood at the edge of the site and shouted at them.

'Go back to school, you wimps!'

'Yeah, how long you gonna collect bones?'

'We gotta get back to work!'

Down at the site, a beautiful young woman with thick blonde hair and large brown eyes stared back at them. Her name was Daisy, and she wore khaki shorts, a white blouse, and an olive-green top with deep pockets for samples. Around her neck was an unusual-looking cone-shaped rock on a leather thong.

Daisy was in charge of the dig. She could see

the tense looks on the students' faces as the builders harassed them.

'Ignore them,' Daisy told the students. 'Don't forget that valuable fossils have been found at this site. The university has a court order preventing these guys from building here until all the fossils have been removed.'

Just then a long black limousine pulled up. The driver hopped out and ran around to the side to open the door. Daisy watched a man with a low forehead and broad shoulders get out. His black hair was slicked back and his black suit was sharply creased.

'Hey, Mr Scapelli!' one of the builders shouted. The others quickly parted as Scapelli stepped to the edge of the excavation site. He stared down at the students and frowned.

'Who's in charge of this hole?' he barked.

Daisy took a deep breath and walked towards him. 'I'm the boss here.'

'I'm Anthony Scapelli,' the man said. 'And I'm the boss elsewhere. My boys need to get back to work. How long you gonna be digging up these bones?'

'As long as our court order lasts, Mr Scapelli,' Daisy replied patiently. 'The university has already explained to you how important this site is. We'll get done sooner if your goons stop harassing us.'

Anthony Scapelli studied her for a moment. 'You look like you know what you're doing,' he said with a knowing smile. 'I'll bet you'll be done by tonight.'

'I doubt that,' Daisy replied, refusing to be bullied.

Anthony Scapelli looked surprised that she'd disagreed. He stepped closer and spoke in a low voice. 'A lot of girls from Brooklyn have been disappearing lately.' He smirked. 'I'd be careful if I were you.'

Before Daisy could reply, Scapelli span around and got back into his limo. Daisy knew a threat when she heard one, and she wasn't about to let that slick-looking thug get away with it. She turned to a young man standing near her.

'I'm going to find a phone and call the university,' she said. 'Keep everyone digging until I get back.'

Daisy walked up the street towards a restaurant where she thought she'd seen a phone box the day before.

Up ahead, two men sat in a parked stolen car. Both had gaunt faces and pale skin with an un-naturally greenish sheen. Their hair was unkempt, and their clothes were so new they still had the price tags on them. The one sitting behind the steering-wheel was named Iggy. He wore a purple jacket with wide pointed lapels, a shiny purple shirt, and a medallion on a chain around his neck. Beside him sat Spike, who wore a grey jacket and a black turtleneck sweater. He also wore a medallion on a chain. They both looked strangely out of place.

For several weeks now, the two had been searching Brooklyn, looking for a particular young woman. They'd already kidnapped several, but they'd turned out to be the wrong ones. These mistakes had created a considerable amount of tension between the two.

'This time you better not blow it,' Iggy said.

'Since when am I the one blowing it?' Spike asked. 'Look at you. Like, you really fit in wearing that ridiculous suit.'

'I look like a regular Brooklynite,' Iggy insisted. '*You're* the one who looks stupid.'

'No, I —' Suddenly Spike noticed someone walking towards them. 'Hey, is that her?'

'Uh, sure it's her.' Iggy squinted uncertainly. 'I mean, she's got two arms, one head, two legs . . .'

'So did the last four girls we kidnapped,' Spike snapped. 'The boss is gonna kill us if we blow it again.'

'We won't blow it,' Iggy said. He shifted the car into gear and put his foot down on the accelerator. *Crunk!* Their car smashed into the car parked in front of them.

'It would be nice if you knew how to drive,' Spike said snidely.

'I know how to drive,' Iggy replied angrily, as he backed their car directly into the car parked behind them. 'Just not one of these.'

Finally Iggy steered the car into the street. Lurching, coughing, and scraping other parked cars, it began to follow Daisy.

Just up the road, in front of the Bella Napoli restaurant, the Mario brothers were having car problems of their own. The van wouldn't start. Mario opened the bonnet and looked at the engine.

'Hand me a spanner, Luigi,' he said, holding out his hand.

Mario felt Luigi put something in his hand, but it wasn't a spanner. It was a glove.

'Hey, Luigi,' he said. 'What's the matter with you?'

Luigi didn't answer. Mario looked up and saw what was wrong. Luigi was staring at a pretty young woman with thick blonde hair who was standing at a phone box on the pavement. She was digging through her pockets for change.

'Hey, listen,' Mario said. 'Either go and talk to that girl or help me out here, OK?'

Luigi seemed to snap out of his daze. Reaching into his pocket for a quarter, he walked over towards her.

Mario watched him go. He hoped Luigi would think of something intelligent to say. His younger brother needed a woman in his life.

Luigi gave the quarter to Daisy, then stood staring at her while she made her call. He couldn't take his eyes off her. She was so pretty.

Daisy hung up and bit her nails worriedly. She couldn't get anyone at the university to agree to more security for the site. And who were those two creeps in the car? Were they following her?

'Uh, you OK?' Luigi stammered.

'I guess so,' Daisy said. 'Thanks for the change.'

Luigi stared down at his shoes. He wanted to keep talking to her, but he didn't know what to say.

'I'm Daisy,' said Daisy.

'That's nice.' Luigi smiled nervously. 'I never met a Daisy before. I mean, I've seen the flowers lots of times . . .' He stopped talking, worried that she might get the wrong impression. 'Uh, not that I hang out in flower shops.'

Over by the van, Mario rolled his eyes. His brother was about as smooth as sandpaper.

'Well, bye,' Daisy said. She looked as if she was going to leave.

'Hey, wait,' Luigi blurted out. 'We have a van.'

Daisy stopped. 'Are you offering me a lift?'

'Well, it's broken,' Luigi admitted with a shrug.

Then he brightened. 'Uh, unless you're going downhill from here. I mean, we could take it out of gear and coast.'

Daisy frowned. Over by the van, Mario groaned. He could see that Luigi was going to lose her if someone didn't come to his rescue.

'The van's fixed,' Mario said as he walked over to them. 'Look, what my brother is trying to say is that he doesn't know what to say because you've got him all mixed up. Just standing near you makes him feel so full of emotion that he doesn't know where to start. The point is, if you believe in love at first sight, get in the van.'

Daisy was a bit shocked by Mario's bluntness, but at least he was honest. And Luigi was cute. And those creeps in the car were making her nervous. She got in the van.

As Mario drove towards the excavation site, Daisy told them a little bit about why she was in Brooklyn digging up dinosaur fossils. But too soon, it seemed, they arrived at the site.

'Well, um, thanks for the lift,' Daisy said. She reached for the door handle, then paused, looking back at Luigi.

'Uh . . . it was a pleasure to meet me. I mean, it was a pleasure to meet you,' he said.

'Hey, Luigi,' Mario said. 'Wasn't there something you wanted to ask Daisy?'

'Huh?'

'About tonight,' Mario hinted. 'Remember Bella Napoli?'

'Oh yeah. Uh . . .' Luigi still couldn't get the words out. Mario sighed.

'My brother was gonna ask you to join us at the Bella Napoli for dinner at eight o'clock,' Mario said. 'He just doesn't want to seem forward.'

'Oh, no, that's all right,' Daisy said quickly. 'Dinner would be nice.'

'Great,' Mario said. 'We'll pick you up at the excavation site, OK?'

'Fine.'

In their apartment that evening, Mario put on a dark shirt. Luigi decided to stay with his hooded sweatshirt. As usual when one of them was nervous about something, they started to argue.

'I'm sick and tired of you running my life,' Luigi said as he combed his hair. 'Don't talk for me anymore.'

Mario pulled on a tan sports jacket. 'If you want to talk for yourself, when you open your mouth, *words* gotta come out.'

'What was I supposed to say,' Luigi asked. 'Hi, princess, I'm a plumber?'

Mario's jaw dropped. 'How dare you talk about

your lifeblood like that? You know what you gotta do? You gotta get some family pride.'

'You always know what I gotta do,' Luigi replied angrily. 'But when it comes to what *you* gotta do, you got no idea.'

Mario stared at his brother. 'What are you talking about?'

'I'm talking about Daniella,' Luigi said. 'You know why you don't ask her to marry you? Because you're afraid she'll turn you down.'

'Suddenly Mr What-words-am-I-gonna-say? is all full of words!' Mario shouted angrily. He turned and started to leave the room. Luigi felt bad.

'Wait, Mario,' he said. 'Come back here. I need to ask you something.'

Mario stopped. 'What?'

'So with this girl, Daisy, what do you think I should do?'

Mario didn't feel so angry any more. 'The first thing you gotta do is tell her what you are. Even if the girl is a princess, their toilets clog up, too, you know.'

5

Daisy was waiting for them at the excavation site. Luigi stumbled out of the van. He looked at Daisy under the streetlights.

'Hi. Uh . . . I wanted to tell you something I didn't get to say before,' he said. 'Basically, I'm a plumber.'

Daisy wasn't certain why he'd told her that. But he was awfully cute.

'That's great,' she said. 'You can never find a plumber when you need one.'

Mario honked the horn.

'Listen,' Luigi said, 'you want to go to eat?'

'Sure,' Daisy answered.

As they entered the van, neither Daisy nor the Mario brothers realized that they were being watched. Across the street, in a broken-down car, were Iggy and Spike.

'She's getting into that van,' Spike said.

'OK,' Iggy answered. 'We'll follow them and get her when she's alone – no matter what.'

Spike nodded. A fly buzzed in the window and landed on the inside of the windscreen. With a flick of his unnaturally long tongue, Spike gobbled it up.

'Hey, what're you doing?' Iggy asked irritably.

'I'm eating,' Spike snapped. 'Can't a guy eat?'

Iggy was about to reply when Mario's van rolled off. Iggy and Spike drove after it.

Murals of Italy adorned the walls of the Bella Napoli restaurant, and a violinist and an accordion player serenaded the diners. Luigi and Daisy sat down with Mario and his girlfriend, Daniella. Mario's girlfriend had black hair and long red fingernails and was wearing a low-cut red and black striped dress.

They ordered dinner and started to chat. Daisy was shy and said little until after dinner when Daniella asked what she did. Daisy told her about working at the excavation site.

'Let me get this straight,' Daniella said. 'Scapelli started blasting this building site, and they found dinosaur bones and *what* in the rocks?'

'Iridium,' Daisy said.

'Unbelievable.' Luigi shook his head in wonder.

Mario turned to him. 'You know what that is?'

'No,' Luigi admitted. 'But how could anything with a name like iridium *not* be important?'

'It means that a meteor may have hit there a

long time ago,' Daisy explained. 'We think that could be what wiped out the dinosaurs.'

'Wow,' Luigi said in awe. 'Dinosaurs in Brooklyn.'

'Relax, Luigi,' Mario said. 'There used to be Dodgers here too.'

It was supposed to be a joke, but Luigi didn't think it was so funny. 'Hey, cool it, Mario. We're talking to the university's head bone-ologist here.'

'Not the head,' Daisy gently corrected him. 'I'm just the only person willing to work the long hours for the little money.'

Just then Daniella spied the cone-shaped stone hanging on the thin leather thong around Daisy's neck. 'Hey, that's an incredible rock. Can I see it?'

'Actually, I don't take it off,' Daisy said. 'I know it's weird, but it's the only thing I've got from when I was found.'

'Found?' Daniella looked puzzled.

'I was abandoned as a baby,' Daisy explained. 'You know St Teresa's on Fulton Street? That's where I was brought up.'

'Wow, so you don't know who your mother and father are, either?' Luigi said.

'What do you mean, "either"?' Daisy asked.

'Mario brought me up,' said Luigi. 'I guess that sort of makes my brother my mother . . . well, my father . . . I mean . . .'

25

'So, what are you kids gonna do tonight?' Daniella asked, trying to change the subject. 'I mean, it's such a nice night for two people . . .'

'And two people – and two people only – are needed to get the van back home,' Mario added. 'So that leaves . . .'

'I can do the maths myself,' Luigi said. He turned to Daisy. 'So, uh, can I walk you home?'

Outside, across the street from the restaurant, Iggy and Spike were waiting in their car. They sat up when the door to the restaurant opened and Mario came out with Daniella.

'Hey look!' Iggy whispered, pointing at Daniella as she walked towards the van with Mario.

'Hair different,' Spike said. 'Clothes different. Different height.'

'Devious,' Iggy said. 'She's wearing a disguise.'

'Yeah, I spotted that right away,' Spike said. 'She thinks just because all these humans look alike, she's gonna fool us.'

'We'll follow them and get her when he drops her off,' Iggy said, starting the car.

Unaware that he was being followed, Mario drove to the block where Daniella lived and dropped her off.

Daniella watched him pull away. Mario was a good man. Solid, concerned for others, and very handy with tools. She turned and was about to go into the building when a hand slid around her mouth. A moment later Iggy and Spike dragged her away.

Back at the Bella Napoli, Luigi and Daisy left the restaurant and stood out on the pavement. It was the first time they'd been alone with each other, and both were feeling awkward.

'Uh, would it be all right if I took your arm?' Luigi asked.

'Uh, OK,' Daisy replied.

'I don't mean actually *take* it,' Luigi explained.

'I know,' Daisy said. 'You meant arm-in-arm.'

'Right,' Luigi said.

'I mean, not *in* arm,' Daisy corrected herself. 'More like arm *over* arm.'

'Yeah,' Luigi agreed. 'I'm not thinking we should, like, swap bones or anything.'

They started to walk along the darkened street. But Luigi was too nervous to stay quiet for long.

'OK,' he said. 'Maybe I'd better apologize now in case I say something really weird.'

'Look, weird is working all day in a bone pit,' Daisy said. 'Then spending your nights reading about things that have been dead for sixty-five million years.'

'Sounds fascinating,' Luigi said, but Daisy didn't hear him.

'Actually,' she went on, 'I'd understand if you wanted to end this now.'

Luigi stopped and turned to her. 'I was going to say the same thing. In fact, if you want to break up, but then feel bad and need to talk to someone about it, you can call me later.'

They stared at each other for a moment, trying to figure out what they'd said.

'You really think this fossil stuff sounds interesting?' Daisy asked, trying to get back on track.

'I think it's incredible,' Luigi said.

He sounded sincere. Daisy had an idea. 'Know what? If you want, I can show you what it's really like.'

'Cool,' Luigi said.

Together they walked to the excavation site. Daisy gave him a torch and picked up one for herself at the site's equipment rack. They entered a dark tunnel at the bottom of the pit.

'While most kids were watching cartoons I was reading about dinosaurs,' Daisy said, aiming her torch beam at the earthen walls of the tunnel. 'I used to make the nuns take me to the Museum of Natural History, and then I wouldn't want to leave. I used to wear them out.'

'There's nothing worse than cranky nuns,' Luigi

said. 'They're more dangerous than roving street gangs.

'I don't understand why, but I've been drawn to this stuff all my life.' Daisy's torch beam traced the walls. 'I feel more at home down here than I do up on the streets.'

'Home, huh? Well, this is a nice place you've got here,' Luigi said as they entered a wider underground cavern. 'Nice view.'

'You know,' Daisy said, studying him, 'you might just be the first person I've ever met who's actually a little weirder than me.'

'Believe me,' Luigi said, 'If there's anything I understand, it's being into things you don't understand.'

'This is where we've found a lot of fossils,' Daisy said. She aimed her torch at the cavern walls. The beam stopped on some bones still pressed into the rock. 'Creatures like this one used to roam the earth. Sometimes I wonder what he was thinking before he died.'

'Probably, "Noooooooooo! I don't want to die!"' Luigi said with a grin.

Daisy moved closer to the fossil, tracing the bones with her torch. 'Look at the proportions of the bones here. The opposable thumb. It's almost as if this monster was trying to be a human being.'

Luigi had stopped looking at the bones. Now

he was looking at Daisy. 'Yeah,' he said as he moved closer. 'Like he was being drawn to something . . .'

Daisy turned around and looked up into Luigi's eyes. Slowly, she raised her lips to meet his.

Clank! A sound from further down the tunnel startled them.

'What's down there?' Luigi asked, peering into the darkness.

'The sump pumps,' Daisy said.

Clank! There it was again. Luigi recognized the sound of metal against pipe. He motioned Daisy to follow him. As they walked quietly down the tunnel they hear scuffling sounds and then steps coming towards them.

Suddenly Luigi pushed Daisy behind a rock. A split second later, Doug and Mike from Scapelli Plumbing jogged past.

'What's going on?' Daisy whispered.

'Shh.' Luigi pressed his finger to his lips. 'Listen.'

Together they heard the sound of water splashing into the tunnel.

'They broke the sump pumps,' Luigi told her. 'They're trying to ruin the excavation.'

'Oh no! Thank God you're here,' Daisy gasped.

Luigi didn't follow. 'What do you mean?'

'Well, you're a plumber, right?'

'Uh, sure,' Luigi said. He'd never worked on a sump pump in his life. 'I know exactly how to handle it. Let's go.'

6

Twenty minutes later they returned to the site with a sleepy-looking Mario. Daisy led the way.

'Down here!' she cried. 'Hurry!'

The water on the pump-room floor was already ankle-deep and rising. Mario splashed through and kneeled next to the silenced sump pumps, surveying the damage.

'Eiler wrench!' he shouted, holding his hand out like a surgeon.

Fwap! Luigi slapped the eiler wrench into his brother's hand. Mario fitted the wrench over a large bolt and held out his hand again. 'Crescent wrench . . . uh, no, make that a Cumberland gauge.'

Fwap! The gauge hit Mario's hand. A moment later Mario held out his hand again. 'Hand!'

Luigi didn't hesitate. He slapped his hand into Mario's and held tight as his brother leaned down into the mud and muck.

'Is that safe?' Daisy asked nervously.

'Piece of cake.' Luigi winked at her. 'My brother knows his stuff.'

They were too busy to notice two faint torch beams coming from deeper in the tunnel. There, a dejected Iggy and Spike trudged up towards the surface.

'Wrong girl again,' Spike groaned. 'How many does that make?'

'Five,' Iggy replied.

'Zero for five,' Spike said. 'What per cent is that?'

They both thought a while.

'I dunno,' Iggy said finally. 'But whatever it is, it ain't good.'

Spike nodded. 'I'm telling you, if we don't find that girl, he's gonna kill us.'

'He won't kill us. He's not that nice.'

Suddenly Iggy grabbed Spike's arm and stopped. His nostrils flared. 'Smell that? Up ahead, It's *her*!'

They turned off their torches and moved stealthily through the darkened tunnel.

Daisy was so busy watching the Mario brothers that she didn't notice they had company.

Thunk! Thunk! Iggy and Spike each cracked a brother on the head. Mario and Luigi slumped unconscious over the sump pumps. Daisy felt two pairs of hands grab her. She kicked and screamed, but Iggy and Spike held her tightly as they dragged her further down into the tunnel.

Luigi opened his eyes and rubbed the sore spot on the back of his neck. He had a throbbing headache. Mario was slumped over the pump beside him, but where was Daisy?

'Daisy!' he shouted, jumping to his feet. 'Daisy!'

There was no answer. Luigi quickly grabbed his brother and helped him up.

'What happened?' Mario asked groggily.

Before Luigi could answer, they heard a cry in the distance. 'Hey! Get that tongue away from me!'

'That's Daisy!' Luigi gasped, pointing up the tunnel. 'Let's go! This way!'

He started to run, but Mario grabbed him. 'No, it's *this* way,' he said, pointing deeper into the tunnel.

'That way?' Luigi looked confused.

'Trust me on this,' Mario assured him. 'I spend my life with my ears to pipes and tubes like this. I know what I'm talking about.'

They started down the tunnel, but soon came to a dead end. The brothers were surrounded by walls of rock on three sides.

'This way, you said.' Luigi glared at Mario. 'Trust you, you said.'

'I could've sworn it came from down here,' Mario said, looking around helplessly.

Then they heard it again, only more distant this time: 'Leave me alone, you reptiles!'

Mario and Luigi stared at each other in disbelief. Daisy's cries seemed to come from inside the rock wall! Luigi walked up to the rock as if he were trying to see through it.

'Are you crazy?' Mario asked.

The rock wall began to ripple. Suddenly Daisy's frightened face appeared in the rock, and her hands reached out towards Luigi.

'Luigi!' she cried.

Luigi and Mario couldn't believe their eyes. Luigi lunged towards the rock to pull Daisy out but managed to grab only the cone-shaped stone hanging around her neck. Then hands of rock reached out and yanked Daisy back in. Luigi pounded his fists against the rock.

The next thing Mario knew, Luigi was sucked right through the rock wall!

'Hey! Luigi! Hey!' Mario started pounding and kicking the rock frantically. *Thwump!* A second later he was sucked in, too.

Mario was tumbling, floating, weightlessly through rainbows of muted colours. Suddenly he landed on something hard and rough. He looked around and found Luigi sitting next to him. They heard scuffling sounds and turned just in time to see Daisy being dragged away by Spike and Iggy.

'There she is!' Luigi shouted, jumping up. 'Come on, Mario. Run!'

A moment later, Luigi and Mario were no longer in the tunnel. Instead, they were on a ramp above a square in some kind of city. There were buildings and streets and crowds of people rushing around.

'No!' Daisy's voice echoed distantly through the air. The brothers raced towards her, but their path was blocked by throngs of people trying to get around a subway tunnel under construction. Finally they lost sight of her. Mario and Luigi stopped and looked around.

'What is this?' Mario asked.

'I don't know,' Luigi replied. 'I ain't been to Manhattan for a couple of weeks.'

Mario noticed that the buildings around them were crumbling and covered with a slimy yellow fungus. 'Looks like this has been a bad couple of weeks,' he said, touching the yellow stuff. 'This is disgusting.'

Suddenly Luigi saw Daisy on the street below being dragged through the crowds by two guys. 'Mario, look! It's Daisy!'

'I remember those two guys,' Mario said. 'They

were hanging around the phone box when Daisy made that call.'

Daisy spotted them. 'Luigi! Mario!' she cried as Iggy and Spike dragged her towards a waiting taxi.

'We're coming!' Luigi shouted.

They tried to run down a stairway, but it was too crowded. Finally Luigi grabbed the ramp railing and tried to vault over it, but it was covered with slippery fungus. He and Mario stumbled over the edge and fell into an empty fountain.

'You OK?' Luigi asked his brother.

'Yeah, fine,' Mario said, patting his rear end. 'I got some padding. What about you?'

'I'm OK,' Luigi said. He was looking up at a giant poster for some guy called Koopa the Environmentalist. Mario climbed out of the fountain.

'You see Daisy?' he asked.

'No,' Luigi said. 'I . . . ahh!' Two creatures were snarling at him from the middle of the fountain. They looked like giant rats crossed with lizards. Luigi jumped out.

'Gee, where are we?' he gasped, realizing now how strange this place really was. Just about every flat surface was covered with brightly coloured graffiti. Steam hissed out of vents and glowing neon signs advertised tattoo parlours, the Boom Boom Bar, and something called thwomp stompers. There were ramps running in every direction, and a huge metal bucket hung by chains over the centre of the square.

A vendor pushed a food cart towards them. As the brothers watched, amazed, he slid a hot, cooked lizard on to a hot dog bun and waved it at them. 'Hey, gents, get your soiled spiny burger here. I got fried tweeter for twenty Koopons. Or maybe you prefer little wigglers. They're only fifteen.'

'Wherever we are, we're gonna have to be real hungry to eat this stuff,' Mario said nervously.

'Maybe it's the Manhattan of the future,' Luigi said. 'Maybe we were just knocked unconscious for a hundred years or something.'

'Or maybe it's the Bronx of today,' Mario replied. 'No wonder they tell you never to go up there.'

Luigi scratched his head. 'Maybe it's . . . a parallel dimension. Like an alternative world to ours, sharing the same space as us, but totally unreachable except by tunnel and then liquid rock.'

Mario stared at Luigi. 'I think you've been playin' too many video games.'

Even Luigi had to shrug. 'I know. It's farfetched.'

Little did he know . . .

7

High in a tower overlooking the city, the man called Koopa stood at a table looking at campaign posters of himself. Although older now than when he had pursued the meteorite piece himself, Koopa was still handsome, with slicked-back blond hair and the self-assured look of a tyrant. He wore a shiny black suit made of some sort of lizard skin, a grey snake-skin tie, and a black shirt.

As he studied the posters a thin, nervous man approached him.

'Excuse me, sir,' the man stammered meekly. 'The people of Dinohattan are growing restless. There's no water, and that fungus is growing everywhere.'

Koopa turned slowly and frowned at him. 'Why are you telling me this?'

'Well, sir, as your campaign adviser I feel it is my responsibility to alert you to what could become a campaign issue.'

Without warning, Koopa grabbed the man's throat and slowly choked him. 'All they can do is complain,' Koopa said scornfully. '"No food! No water!" They have no *vision*!'

He let go and his campaign adviser dropped to the floor. An attractive woman with red hair entered the room and stepped over the body. She wore a tight black and white dress and a silver necklace with matching earrings. Her name was Lena.

'They just don't get it, darling,' she said.

Koopa looked in disgust at the hand he'd used to choke his campaign adviser. 'He touched my hand with his throat.'

'Oh, you poor boy.' Lena took him by the wrist and led him towards a copper vat filled with boiling wax. Koopa quickly dipped his hand into the wax and pulled it out. Lena pursed her lips and tenderly blew on Koopa's fingers to cool them.

'For sixty-five million years our people have been exiled to this pithole of a sub-dimension,' Koopa said angrily, 'while *mammals* have roamed freely on the other side. But soon that world will be mine.'

'You'll merge the dimensions,' Lena said as she gently peeled the cooled wax off his hand. 'And we'll have everything we've dreamed of. All we need is the meteorite piece.'

'And the princess,' Koopa added. 'I need the princess.'

That wasn't what Lena wanted to hear. 'I know what you really need,' she cooed with a seductive smile.

She had started to lead him towards the bedroom when a door swung open. Iggy and Spike stumbled into the room.

'Oh, uh, sorry, sir,' Iggy said.

'Hello, morons,' Lena said snidely.

Spike straightened up and smiled. 'Oh, hello.'

'Sir,' Iggy said excitedly, 'I've got the princess. She's here, being defungussed.'

'I'm the one who dragged her through the gateway,' Spike said, stepping in front of Iggy.

'Well, I recognized her,' Iggy said, shoving Spike out of the way. 'Spike couldn't tell one human from another.'

'Yes, yes,' Koopa said impatiently. 'And what about the rock?'

'Rock, sir?' Iggy frowned.

'That's right, frog-brain, where is it?' Spike yelled at his partner. Then he turned to Koopa. 'Iggy's always forgetting things. Now, exactly what rock are we talking about?'

Koopa grabbed Spike by the throat and started to squeeze. 'The piece of meteorite she wears around her neck! I told you not to forget it!'

'Bad Spike.' Iggy wagged a finger at his partner. Koopa let go of Spike and glared at him.

'I told *you* to remind him!' he shouted. 'Without that piece, the entire meteorite remains dormant, and I cannot merge the dimensions, which means we're trapped in this world, without access to the resources of the other, which means the very end of the dinosaurs, the greatest creatures to roam the earth! Now, *where* is it?'

Spike and Iggy stared at each other blankly as their walnut-sized brains struggled to remember. Suddenly they brightened and spoke in unison. 'The plumbers took it!'

Koopa stared at him in disbelief. 'What plumbers?'

'At the gateway,' Iggy said.

'Put out an all-points trawl!' Koopa shouted. 'Get me those plumbers!'

Mario and Luigi sat on the kerb in Koopa Square, feeling dejected. Around his neck, Luigi wore Daisy's cone-shaped stone. Behind him, a piece of fungus-covered brick fell from a crumbling building. Luigi picked a small mushroom out of the fungus, toyed with it for a second, then tossed it away.

'I can't believe we lost her.' Luigi moped.

'I know, kid,' Mario nodded sympathetically.

An old lady walked up and stopped in front of them. 'You guys from out of town?' she asked.

'Brooklyn,' Mario said.

The old lady frowned. Apparently she'd never heard of it. 'You're in a dangerous part of town, boys,' she warned them. 'You shouldn't wander around here without a weapon. Do you have one?'

'No.' Mario shook his head.

'Good.' The old lady pulled her own weapon out of her coat. 'Give me all your money.'

In a flash she had their wallets and was tossing dollar bills on the ground.

'Hey!' Mario yelled. 'That's thirty-three bucks.'

'I need Koopons, you lame-brains,' he snapped, and tossed the wallet away. She stared at Daisy's cone-shaped stone around Luigi's neck.

'Well, that ought to do just fine,' she cackled as she reached for it.

Luigi started to back away. 'No! You can't have this. It's not even mine!'

Zap! The old lady aimed and shot her weapon. Luigi reeled back as if stung by a cattle prod. The old lady grabbed the stone and started to race away.

She didn't get far. A large, tough-looking woman wearing a spiky red jacket grabbed the old lady, held her upside down, and shook her.

Jewels, coins, and Daisy's rock clattered on to the pavement. Then the woman tossed the old lady out into the heavy traffic. *Screech!*

Mario and Luigi watched in horror and amazement. As the big woman bent down to pick up her loot, Mario marched up to her.

'All right, lady,' he said. 'It is "lady", isn't it?'

'The name's Bertha,' the woman replied in a deep voice.

'OK, Bertha,' Mario said, 'hand over that stone.'

Bertha just smiled. 'Come get it, big boy.'

Before Mario could make a move, Bertha reached down to her shoes. They looked like big red plastic ski boots with silver cylinders in the back. Mario and Luigi heard a hissing sound, followed by a series of beeps.

Schwoom! The shoes catapulted Bertha into the air, over the traffic to the other side of the street.

The brothers were still watching in wonder when a street musician strolled up to them, strumming a strange instrument. He wore a black T-shirt, a purple waistcoat, and beads.

'Hey, how about a song?' he asked, and then started to play:

> *We got no food anywhere.*
> *We got no water, got no air.*

Got no resources, we're in a stupor.
The fault of course is evil King Koopa . . .

Out of nowhere a siren wailed and a police car skidded up to the kerb. Two big mean-looking police officers got out and started hitting the musician.

'You know the law, Toad!' one of them shouted as he smashed the musician in the head.

'Hey, what's going on?' Mario asked. 'Can't a guy sing?'

'Not anti-Koopa songs, he can't,' the second police officer said. Then he squinted at Mario. 'Hey, you two ain't the plumbers, are you?'

'He is,' Luigi answered with a gulp. 'I'm just apprenticing. Why?'

The police officers answered by smashing the Mario brothers with their truncheons and arresting them.

A few minutes later Toad and the Mario brothers were dragged through the doors of Metro Central, the main Dinohattan police station. They were brought before a tough-looking police officer named Simon.

'Last name,' Simon said, writing on an arrest form.

'Mario,' said Mario.

'First name,' Simon said.

'Mario,' said Mario.

Simon looked up and frowned. 'Mario Mario?'

'Right,' replied Mario.

Simon shook his head and turned to Luigi. 'What's your name?'

'Luigi,' said Luigi.

'Luigi Luigi?' Simon asked.

'No,' said Luigi. 'Luigi Mario.'

Simon nodded. 'Glad we got that straight. Now take 'em to the defungus room.'

Mario and Luigi were led down a corridor and into a room lined with stainless steel walls. Toad was already in there. They were surrounded by men wearing gas masks. One of them grabbed Mario and started to pull his trousers open.

'Hey!' Mario shouted. 'I don't even let my girlfriend do this!'

The man ignored him and shoved a thick hose into his trousers. Nearby, Luigi was getting the same treatment.

'Ow! Whoa!' he shouted. 'Come on, I'm ticklish down there.'

The hoses blasted white powder into their trousers.

'What's going on?' the brothers shouted in unison.

'Defungus,' Toad explained. 'There's fungus choking the whole city. Horrible stuff. Takes all our water. It's everywhere.'

The men wearing gas masks stepped out of the room. Suddenly nozzles in the walls started spraying a medicinal-smelling yellow liquid. The prisoners were drenched with it. Then they were forced into another room where huge turbines created powerful winds.

'This is the drying room!' Toad shouted over the roar.

Once dry, the three prisoners were taken to the detention area and led past crowded cells filled with nasty reptilian-looking prisoners.

Finally, the brothers and Toad were thrown into a cell of their own. Toad immediately burst into song:

> *Sitting in cramped detention*
> *With plumbers from another dimension . . .*

He paused and frowned. 'Hey, either of you two guys know another word that rhymes with dimension?'

'Yeah,' grumbled Mario. 'Tension. And right now I'm full of it.'

'Wait a minute,' Luigi said to Toad. 'What did you mean by another dimension? Like our worlds have crossed over or something?'

'Give me a break from that tabloid nonsense,' Mario groaned.

'Your brother's right,' Toad said to Mario.

'According to our history, a long time ago a meteor hit this planet and blasted it into parallel universes.'

'You mean, like you bang your head real hard and it makes you see double?' Luigi asked.

'Exactly,' Toad said.

'And that's exactly what's happened to the two of you,' Mario snapped.

Toad ignored him and turned to Luigi. 'Know what else I think? All that fungus is our old king. He's been de-evolved into fungus, and how he's trying to wreak revenge on the city.'

Mario gave Luigi a look that said he thought Toad was nuts.

'Hey,' Luigi chastised his brother. 'Just mellow out, OK?'

'Mellow out?' Mario repeated, amazed. 'You want me to mellow out? OK, I'm mellow.' Mario jumped up, grabbed Luigi by the collar, and screamed, 'We're in this mess because you wanted to save a girl you hardly even know!'

'You said I should go after her.' Luigi squirmed out of his brother's grip.

'I was talking about going on a date!' Mario yelled. 'Not going into another dimension!'

'Aha!' Luigi pointed a finger at his brother. 'Then you do think we're in another dimension!'

'NO, I DON'T!' Mario shouted back. 'I was just using it as part of an argument.'

48

'If Daniella were here you'd want to find her,' Luigi insisted.

'Daniella wouldn't be so stupid as to let herself get brought to a place like this,' Mario shouted back.

'Look, what's your problem?' Luigi asked.

'You really want to know?' Mario asked. '*You're* my problem. My whole life I've been taking care of you.'

'Taking care of me?' Luigi gasped. 'Hey, I never asked.'

'Doesn't matter,' Mario said. 'I promised Pop I'd take care of you and the business. Well, I'm failing at both, and I'm sick of it!'

Suddenly Toad broke into song:

> *Sittin' in a cell with two brothers,*
> *Listenin' to them share with each other . . .*

Both Mario and Luigi gave him a look and he shut up. A second later they hard someone shout, 'Mario brothers?'

Mario jumped to his feet and grabbed the cell's bars. The police officer named Simon was coming down the corridor.

'Yeah,' Mario shouted. 'That's us! And we want a lawyer to get us out of this chicken coop!'

'You got one,' Simon replied.

In a matter of moments the brothers found

themselves sitting at a table in a small black room. The door opened, and Koopa entered, wearing a black suit with a white shirt and a maroon tie. He wanted them to think he was a lawyer.

'Boys, boys!' Koopa exclaimed grandly as he extended his hand. 'How's prison treating you? Excuse me for saying this, but you look like hell. I'm Larry Lazard, your lawyer.'

Mario shook his hand. The minute they'd finished, Koopa extended his hand to Simon, who quickly sprayed it with disinfectant.

'Who sent you?' Mario asked. 'You from the city?'

'I'm from that little part of all of us that can't stand to see someone else in need or pain,' Koopa said, sitting down opposite them.

'Yeah, sure,' Mario said. 'So who's this Koopa clown? His stupid name's all over the place. We wanna see that goofball *now*.'

'I don't think you want to do that,' Koopa said with a raised eyebrow. He leaned over the table and whispered, 'This Koopa "clown" is one mean, evil, egg-sucking son of a snake.'

Mario and Luigi glanced at each other nervously.

'So. Where's the meteorite piece?' Koopa asked.

'The what?' Luigi scowled.

Koopa lunged forward and grabbed Luigi by

the neck. 'You know what I'm talking about?' he shouted.

Mario jumped up and grabbed Koopa. 'Let go of him!' he yelled. 'If anyone's gonna wring Luigi's neck, it's gonna be me!'

Simon pulled Mario away. 'No one touches King Koopa,' he said.

'You're Koopa!' exclaimed Mario.

'But you said . . .' started Luigi.

'One evil, egg-sucking son of a snake,' said Koopa. 'Did I lie?'

Koopa let go of Luigi and turned to Simon, who quickly disinfected him again. 'Take them to the de-evolution chamber,' he muttered.

8

In the centre of the de-evolution chamber was a silver chair. Above it was a device that looked like a space satellite. Toad was already there when Simon brought Luigi and Mario in.

'You think I'm scared?' Toad asked. 'I'm not scared.'

A guard threw him into the chair. Metal bands automatically clamped down on his wrists and ankles.

'Help!' he screamed. 'Don't do it!'

A door opened and Koopa entered the room.

'You! Koopa!' Toad shouted. 'You're a lousy king!'

Koopa shook his head as if he was disappointed. 'One thing I cannot stand is disrespect. Simon!'

'Yes sir!' Simon snapped to attention.

Koopa pointed at Toad. 'De-evolve him!'

Trembling with fear, Toad still managed to

mutter: 'Our old king – you thought you could get rid of him, but you couldn't . . .'

'See you later, alligator.' Koopa waved at him. The chair slid backwards on a track, and then slowly rose until it was covered by the large satellite device. Koopa turned to Mario and Luigi, who were still being restrained by the guards. 'You may understand evolution as an upward process. Things evolve from primeval slime to single-celled organisms up to intelligent life.'

As Koopa spoke, he walked towards a control panel. 'De-evolution works in the opposite way . . . to simpler, less intelligent forms of life. Thanks to this machine, even our most restless citizens can become faithful members of my elite guard of goombas.'

Koopa flicked a switch, and the machine around Toad began to glow and make a hissing sound. After a moment it stopped and the chair descended again. Where Toad had sat, now sat a goomba.

'Why did you do that to him?' Luigi shouted.

'Yeah,' yelled Mario. 'What single-celled organism did *you* evolve from?'

'Me?' Koopa smiled. 'Tyrannosaurus rex, the lizard king, thank you very much. But though my evolution was wonderful and sweet, your de-evolution will be a living nightmare . . . Unless you tell me where that piece of meteorite is.'

The brothers still refused to answer. Koopa smirked and turned to his newest goomba, whom a black-suited technician was helping out of the de-evolution chair.

'So loyal.' Koopa beamed proudly. 'So lethal. So stupid ...' He patted the goomba on the shoulder. 'Walk tall. Be proud. Go, goomba!'

Near him, the technician sneezed. Koopa pushed him into the de-evolution chair. 'You're sick. You better sit down.'

The metal cuffs automatically closed around the stunned technician's ankles and wrists.

'We can't have you spreading germs around,' Koopa said as he strolled back to the control panel.

'But ... but ...' the technician gasped in protest.

Once again the de-evolution machine dropped over the chair. With an evil smile on his face, Koopa turned to Mario and Luigi. 'Millions of years of climbing up from the ooze, instantly reversed. Imagine the horror as it all slips away. It's worse than mere death. It's being undone.'

The king turned the intelligence dial to Primordial. As the de-evolution machine hissed, Koopa's smile disappeared.

'You mammals stole our world,' he ranted at the brothers. 'Dinosaurs were the greatest crea-

tures to roam the earth. Mammals were just shrews
. . . mice. They didn't even dare peek out from
under a leaf when the dinosaurs came by.'

Koopa stared at Mario and Luigi. 'One last
time. Where is the rock?'

Luigi glanced at Mario and silently shook his
head.

The de-evolution machine stopped hissing and
rose. All that remained of the technician was a
puddle of greenish ooze. Koopa stared at the
dripping mess in disgust.

'All right.' Koopa nodded grimly. 'Which one of
you wants to go first?'

Mario and Luigi looked around. Simon was
aiming some kind of ray gun at them. Goombas
guarded the doors. There was no way to escape.
The brothers stepped towards Koopa at the same
time.

'I'll go,' Mario volunteered.

'Take me,' said Luigi.

Koopa narrowed his eyes.

Suddenly Luigi nodded at Mario, and together
they pushed the king into his own de-evolution
chair. The restraints automatically slapped down
on Koopa's ankles and wrists, and the de-evolution
machine began to drop.

'You're going back to where you came from,
lizard!' Mario shouted triumphantly.

'Help me!' cried Koopa, now sitting in the puddle of primordial ooze that had once been the technician. Simon and the guards dashed towards him. In the confusion, Mario and Luigi escaped out of the door.

'Get this filthy gunk off me!' Koopa screamed. 'Get those plumbers! Run me a bath!'

Simon managed to turn off the de-evolution machine and help Koopa out of the chair, but not before the de-evolution process had begun. There was a glimmer in one of Koopa's eyes, and for a moment the skin around it became scaly and reptilian. Koopa slapped a hand to his eye. 'I'll kill those plumbers,' he growled.

Alarm bells rang loudly and sirens wailed. Outside the de-evolution room, Mario and Luigi ran down a fungus-covered breeze-block corridor, chased by goombas shooting fireballs.

Crack! A fireball hit the wall above them, carving out a huge chunk of masonry. Mario grabbed Luigi and ducked around a corner. Luigi stared at the wall. A mushroom was growing out of it.

'Mario, look at this,' he said in wonder. 'A mushroom growing in the fungus.'

'Luigi,' Mario replied, ducking another fireball. 'Mushrooms *are* fungi. Leave it alone!'

'Hey, what's that?' Luigi pointed at a small, black metal ball with a wind-up key sticking out of it. It had just popped out of a crack in the wall.

Luigi watched it drop down and roll on to the floor.

'Looks kind of like a bomb,' he said.

'Come on!' Mario cried as a fireball almost took his head off. He grabbed Luigi, and they jumped over a railing and slid on a nearby winch. They landed in front of five metal doors.

'What do we do now?' Mario gasped. The footsteps of the goombas were growing louder behind them.

'My instincts tell me to pick this one.' Luigi pointed at the second door.

'Then we're going through *this* one!' Mario grabbed his brother and pushed through the fourth door.

They stumbled into an underground car-park for police cars. Long antennae from the cars reached up to an electric power grid in the ceiling. The brothers ducked between the cars just seconds before the door flew open and half a dozen police officers burst in. While the police officers spread out to search for them, Mario and Luigi quietly opened the door of one of the cruisers.

Inside, they found themselves staring at a strange dashboard filled with unfamiliar dials and gauges.

'OK,' Mario said, settling in behind the

controls. 'First, we're stealing this thing. Second, *I'm* driving.'

'I'll look at the map,' Luigi said, pressing some buttons and quickly booting up a colourful map on a small computer screen. Mario watched in amazement.

'I can't believe you did that,' he gasped.

'It comes from sitting on my bottom all day, playing video games,' Luigi replied with a shrug.

Mario reached towards the dashboard and flicked a few switches, but nothing happened. Outside in the car-park the heavily armed police officers were coming closer.

'Hurry!' Luigi hissed.

'I'm hurrying,' Mario replied as he broke into a sweat. 'Only *I* don't play video games all day!'

Finally he hit the right switch, and the car roared to life. 'Let's hit the bricks!' Mario shouted, pressing on the accelerator.

A shower of sparks burst from the electric grid above them as the car wheel-spinned. Drawn to the sound, the police officers aimed their weapons and fired. Bright orange fireballs whizzed past the escaping police car.

Mario steered the car towards an up-ramp, praying it would lead to an exit.

A second later they shot out into the night, careering through the heavy traffic.

'Find the siren!' Mario shouted.

Luigi started punching buttons. One of them activated the radio. A voice blared out: 'Alien species escaping from Metro Central. Use of unreasonable force is recommended.'

'Holy cow!' Luigi gasped. 'Don't tell me we gotta deal with aliens, too!'

'I got news for you,' Mario shouted. '*We're* the aliens.'

'We are?' The look of surprise on Luigi's face turned into a smile. 'Hey, Mario! Remember "Man Discovers He's an Alien!"? You said it couldn't happen.'

'Yeah, well, man is about to discover he's goomba food if we don't hightail it outta here,' said Mario.

The police car skidded through an intersection, narrowly missing a head-on collision with a large rubbish truck. Now they heard two loud, wailing sirens. A second later, police cars raced up on either side of them. Police officers rolled down their windows and aimed their weapons at the stolen car.

Mario jammed on the brakes and skidded to a stop just as both police fired.

Ka-boom! The two police cars blew each other up. As jagged motor parts rained down on them, Mario quickly accelerated the stolen police car again.

'Now, *this* is driving!' he shouted with glee.

Once again, the radio crackled on: 'Aliens heading west on Great Koopa Boulevard. Approaching Grand Koopa Parkway near the turn-off to the Koopahari Desert Tunnel.'

'And I thought Kennedy had a lot of stuff named after him,' Mario grumbled. Ahead, illuminated by the car's headlights, the brothers could see that the road forked. One sign read: Grand Koopa River Parkway. The other said: Koopahari Desert Tunnel. But the entrance to the tunnel was blocked by a black and yellow barrier and a sign that read:

Danger! Tunnel Unfinished!

'Which way?' Mario shouted.

'You really want my opinion?' Luigi asked. Mario nodded. 'OK, definitely the parkway.'

Mario veered towards the tunnel.

'Ha!' Luigi laughed. 'Just like I figured. I wanted the tunnel so I said the parkway, because I knew you'd go the opposite way. I'm on to you Mario.'

A second later their police car smashed through the barrier. The power coil on its roof was sheared off, and they coasted silently into the dark tunnel.

Mario (right) and Luigi, Brooklyn's best plumbers.

Luigi and Daisy explore the tunnel beneath the archaeological dig.

The sprawling city of Dinohattan awaits Mario and Luigi at the far end of the tunnel.

Dinohattan is a dangerous place—even an old lady will rob you if you give her a chance.

King Koopa, disguised as a lawyer, questions Mario and Luigi closely.

Daisy is escorted to Koopa's chambers by Hark, a goomba.

Princess Daisy, imprisoned, is comforted by the royal pet, Yoshi.

Iggy (right) and Spike are brought before Koopa by two of his goomba henchmen.

Mario and the missing girls from Brooklyn escape down a frozen ventilation shaft on a mattress-turned-sled.

Lena climbs to the top of the meteor to replace the missing piece.

Luigi, Daisy, and the others look on in fear as Lena attempts to merge the dimensions.

Koopa feels the effects of the merge.

9

In his tower suite high above the city, Koopa relaxed in a steaming bath of greenish-brown mud. Across from him, Lena slid into the marble tub.

'There's nothing like a mud bath,' Lena sighed sensuously. 'It's clean and dirty at the same time.'

'Hush, I'm thinking,' Koopa replied.

'About the merge,' Lena guessed. 'You don't really believe only your princess can do it, do you?' She slid through the mud and rubbed against him. 'I think we can do it, together.'

Koopa wasn't interested in what she thought. 'Nobody's merging with anybody until I have that meteorite piece!' he snapped irritably. 'We need the princess. She's the only one who can withstand the force of the meteorite. She was born to do it.'

'Oh? And what am I?' Lena asked jealously.

Chopped lizard? Think of *me*, Koopa. We've been together since before she was hatched!'

Ignoring her, Koopa pressed a button. A moment later, Spike stumbled into the room.

'Where are the plumbers?' Koopa asked.

'In the Koopahari Tunnel, sir,' Spike replied. 'Heading for the desert.'

'Hmm.' Koopa thought for a second. 'Then it's bye-bye, plumbers. The tunnel ends in a two-hundred-foot drop to the desert floor, so I guess we'll just pick through the remains. A bit gruesome, perhaps, but I'll still get what I want.'

The king snapped his fingers. 'Get us our robes, Spike.' He watched the goon retrieve the robes from a cupboard and return. 'Tell me, Spike, have you been spending much time in the de-evolution machine?'

'Oh, no, sir,' Spike replied. Then he bent close to Koopa's ear and whispered, 'The only time I go near it is to pull Iggy out. Between you and me, sir, I'm not sure I really need Iggy any more. I'm carrying him so much, you may as well just have one of us.'

'I'll make that decision,' Koopa replied. Then he shouted, 'Iggy!'

The door opened and Iggy came in. 'Yes, sir?'

'Any minute now the plumbers will plummet to their deaths,' Koopa said.

'Hence the name *plumbers*, I guess,' Iggy said with a grin. He waited for the others to laugh, but no one reacted. Iggy coughed. 'Spike told me that joke, sir.'

'I need you two to go out to the desert, get me the meteorite piece, and mop up a bit,' Koopa ordered.

'Mop up the desert?' Spike scowled. 'Is that a figure of speech, sir?'

Koopa groaned. Iggy winked at him and pointed at Spike's head to indicate how dumb Spike was. But Koopa had had enough. 'You two, come with me,' he ordered.

'What about me?' Lena asked.

'You bring me the princess,' Koopa snapped. 'Have her cleaned up.'

'Very well, *sir*,' Lena replied with a bow. She was not at all pleased.

A few moments later, Koopa led Spike and Iggy into the de-evolution chamber. Without a word he pushed Spike into the chair and watched as the restraints clamped down.

'Wha –?' Spike gasped. 'What are you doing?'

Koopa said nothing as the chair slid back and the de-evolution machine dropped over the goon's head. Iggy stood beside the king, smiling.

'Wise choice, sir,' he said. 'Spike will be much better off as dripping goo.'

Koopa stepped to the control panel and turned

the intelligence dial from Primordial past Neutral to Advanced.

'What are you doing?' Iggy gasped.

The machine glowed and hissed. Moments later the device rose. Spike appeared to be sitting straighter, with his legs crossed in a debonair fashion. There was a new clarity in his eyes.

'Hello, not-so-benevolent dictator,' Spike greeted Koopa. 'That's a charming ensemble. Should come back into style some time this epoch.'

'Is that you, Spike?' Iggy asked, amazed.

Spike turned and looked down his nose at his partner. 'Good day, peasant.'

'Now you!' Koopa grabbed Iggy and threw him into the de-evolution chair. 'Maybe if you're not such idiots, you won't mess up this time.'

A few moments later Iggy was similarly evolved.

'My word,' he said, stepping out of the chair. 'You don't say. I feel as though I've been transformed.'

'Yes,' Spike agreed. 'A most agreeable transmogrification.'

'Enough of this rubbish!' Koopa shouted with a sweep of his arm. 'To the desert, both of you!'

Iggy didn't move. 'It hardly seems logical for us to do such menial labour, does it? Perhaps we should stay and help formulate strategy, *tête-à-tête*, inner circle, that sort of thing.'

Koopa gritted his teeth, wondering if he'd made a mistake by giving these idiots brains. 'Listen,' he barked. 'Here's what seems logical to me. If you do *not* return with the meteorite piece, I will personally kill you both.'

'Since you put it that way,' Spike said, pushing his partner towards the door.

'Yes,' Iggy agreed. 'Uh, very good point. Interesting syllogism. I think it works on numerous levels.'

The door closed. Idiots! Koopa thought.

The stolen police car soared silently through the dark tunnel. Long tendrils of yellow fungus blew in through the car's smashed front windscreen. While Luigi wiped the stuff from his face, Mario pumped desperately on the brakes.

'I can't stop this thing!' he shouted. 'And I can't see where I'm going! This fungus is gonna kill us!'

Ahead, through the thick, web-like fungus, Luigi could see a small circle of dim light growing larger. Suddenly he realized what it was.

'Look out, Mario!' he screamed. 'We're hitting the end of the tunnel!'

Too late! They shot out of the tunnel's end and

into the night air like a spitball. The sandy desert floor below raced up towards them at a blinding speed. Mario and Luigi covered their eyes with their hands. This was the end. It was all over. They were going to . . .

Sproing! Just inches from the desert floor, the car suddenly stopped and shot back into the sky, as if attached to a giant bungee cord. Down again it plunged. Only this time the car came to a gentle stop on the desert floor.

'Aha!' Mario shouted gleefully, still gripping the wheel. 'Talk about superior driving skills!'

Seated beside him, Luigi was staring down at a tiny piece of fungus in his hand.

'Come on, let's get out,' Mario said. The brothers crawled out on to the cool sands of the desert. In the moonlight, Luigi stared back up at a long, thick tendril of fungus that stretched from the tunnel opening down to the back of the car.

'Wow,' Luigi said in awe. 'What's the deal with this fungus?'

Mario shook his head. 'Nothing.'

'I'm telling you, Mario,' Luigi said, staring up again at the fungus. 'There's something going on here. I'm serious.'

'There's nothing going on,' Mario insisted. 'Superior driving skills. Full stop.'

*

Back in Koopa's tower, Daisy sat with Daniella and several other girls in a large concrete cell guarded by a goomba. The girls had all been abducted by Iggy and Spike. Daniella was filling Daisy in on what little she knew.

'All I know is some guy named Koopa is looking for some princess or something,' Daniella said as she chewed on a stick of gum she'd got from one of the other girls.

'So why are all of you here?' Daisy asked.

Daniella shrugged. 'Those goons who kidnapped us thought we were the princess. Supposedly this princess went through some kind of gateway.'

'Gateway to what?' Daisy asked. When Daniella shrugged, Daisy turned to a short girl named Angelica, who was dressed in a turquoise cocktail dress.

'I don't know and I don't care,' Angelica replied. 'I just want to get out of here.'

Daisy was just about to ask another question when Lena came in.

'Who are you?' Daniella asked.

'Where are we?' asked Angelica.

'You can't keep us here,' Daisy insisted.

'Girls, girls, please,' Lena replied. 'Trust me, I don't want you here, either.'

'Are you here to help us?' Daniella asked as Lena slowly studied each one of them.

'Hardly,' Lena replied. 'Let me guess. Which one of you is Princess Daisy?'

Lena stopped in front of Daisy and stared hard. A small, tight smile appeared on the woman's face. 'Ah yes. You have your mother's eyes.'

The next thing Daisy knew, Lena escorted her out of the cell to a dressing-room, where her hair was done and she was dressed in a lavender gown. Then Lena took her up in a lift to Koopa's suite. As they entered the room, Daisy heard a strange animal sound, but she was too distracted to pay attention.

'Would you like to see your mother?' Lena asked.

'Yes, of course,' Daisy gasped, looking around. 'Where is she?'

'In the ground somewhere, I suppose,' Lena replied, enjoying the shocked and saddened look on Daisy's face. 'She's dead.'

Daisy looked down at the floor. Lena had no patience for such self-pity. 'Listen, princess. I've been hanging around Koopa as long as that meteorite piece has been hanging around your neck. And if you want to *keep* that neck . . .'

Before she could continue, the door swung open, and Koopa entered. As his eyes focused on Daisy, a smile crept across his lips. Lena quickly rose and headed for the door.

'Why, Koopa . . .' She smiled as she passed him. 'I was just telling Daisy about her mother.'

Koopa gazed at Daisy and shook his head wistfully. 'It was sad about your mother. She was an inspiration . . . until she got in my way.'

'What about my father?' Daisy asked. 'Is he still alive?'

Koopa moved closer to her. 'Yes. No. Maybe.'

'Which?' Daisy asked with a frown. 'Where is he?'

Koopa moved closer, still staring at her intensely. 'Here . . . and there.'

As Daisy gazed back into the king's eyes, she began to feel light-headed. She quickly looked away. 'Stay away from me.'

'Don't fight it,' Koopa whispered, coming still closer. 'You know you're drawn to it. Always searching for your past and where you really belong. You belong here. Now. With me.'

Daisy felt her will to resist him slowly fading away.

Grrrr! The spell was broken by a growl. Daisy was shocked to see a baby dinosaur bounding towards her. It looked just like a miniature Tyrannosaurus rex! The creature stopped just a foot from Daisy and stared back at her.

'You can pat him,' Koopa said. 'His name is Yoshi. He's one of a long line of royal pets.'

Fascinated, Daisy reached out towards the tiny beast. Yoshi quickly rolled on to his back so that she could pat his stomach.

'He's real,' Daisy gasped.

'You see?' Koopa said, sliding close to her again. 'You're one of us. Descended from dinosaurs and destined to rule. You and I, together.' Once again he began to weave a spell upon her. Daisy felt herself growing helpless as his eyes became reptilian and his skin grew scaly. 'You know what they say about little girls,' he hissed softly. 'They never forget the first time they kiss a lizard.'

Koopa seemed to be regressing back into a reptile. He flicked his long tongue at her. Daisy blinked. 'No!' she cried, backing away. 'No! Stop!'

'Uh, excuse us, Koopa?' a voice said.

Daisy looked up and saw Iggy and Spike, the two goons who'd kidnapped her. Koopa became human again and glared at them.

'Catch you at a bad time?' Spike asked.

'We sent a drone to the desert to check on the plumbers,' Iggy reported. 'The plumbers' vehicle is unpeopled.'

'Unpeopled?' Koopa scowled. 'What are you saying?'

'The car is empty,' Iggy explained. 'That would leave one to assume that the plumbers are alive in the desert somewhere.'

Koopa jumped up. 'Then get them, you idiots! If I see you or the plumbers again without the meteorite piece, I'll kill all four of you!'

'Right away, sir!' Iggy and Spike quickly departed, closing the door behind them. Koopa turned back to Daisy.

'I apologize for my slithering manner,' he said, moving towards her again. 'But I need to attend to my evil, ruthless, despotic, world-dominating plan.' He shrugged offhandedly. 'You know how it is.'

'Don't touch me,' Daisy gasped, backing away.

Suddenly Yoshi growled at Koopa, who stopped and stared at the creature with an evil frown. 'See? Even he's loyal to the royal family.' Without warning, he gave the tiny Tyrannosaurus rex a vicious kick and then left the room. Daisy crept over to the little dinosaur and started to pat it again. Royal family? Princess? Was it really possible?

10

It was morning. The hot desert sun had come up. There was nothing to drink, nothing to eat – nothing but sand. The Mario brothers trudged along with no idea of where they were headed.

'I said the parkway,' Luigi said irritably, tired of Mario blaming him for everything that went wrong.

'But you wanted the tunnel,' Mario answered. Meanwhile, Luigi stopped to look around as if trying to decide which way to go.

'Go ahead,' Mario shouted. 'Pick a direction. Over there looks good. We could die there. No, wait! "I got a good feeling" *that's* where we should die, *over there*. Or maybe if we get lucky, we can make it all the way back to Koopaland and *then* get killed!'

Luigi was getting tired of his brother's sarcasm. He trudged up to the top of a nearby ridge to get a better look. In the distance, a small island of buildings and smog rose out of the endless desert. The tallest buildings were two towers, like the World Trade Center. Koopa's towers, Luigi thought.

Mario joined him at the top of the ridge. 'I could've been home with Daniella,' he grumbled, 'watching the Knicks.'

Luigi stared at his brother in disbelief. 'You hate the Knicks.'

'I like 'em now!' Mario shouted.

'OK, fine,' Luigi replied. 'It's all my fault. This is dump on little brother day. Well, I'm sorry we followed Daisy. I'm sorry I fell for her. I'm sorry I got feelings and desires. I'm sorry they stabbed us, defungussed us, choked us, and poked us. It's all my fault. I made them do it to you, Mario. I made 'em evil. I even invented sand.'

Luigi bent down and scooped up some sand in his hand. Mario did the same.

'Yeah? Well, good thinking!' Mario shouted, and threw his handful at Luigi. '*Great* thinking. Now, eat some!'

Luigi threw sand back at Mario. A sand war broke out as they hurled handfuls at each other. Suddenly a six-wheeled dune buggy bounced over the ridge and smashed into a dune, spilling out Iggy and Spike.

'It's those creeps who stole Daisy!' Luigi

shouted. The brothers instantly turned their rage on the dazed former goons and wrestled them to the sand. Pulling his plumber's snake out of his tool belt, Mario tied them up. Bound back-to-back, Iggy and Spike squirmed on the hot sand.

'Ruffians!' Spike shouted. 'Hoodlums!'

'Hooligans!' Iggy added. 'Brigands! Picaroons!'

'We're plumbers!' Mario shouted back.

'Where's Daisy?' Luigi asked.

The former goons glanced at each other and pursed their lips.

Mario pulled a spanner out of his tool belt and waved it at them. 'Start talking, or I'll break your elbow joints.'

'She's in the tower,' Iggy said.

Mario dragged the two ex-goons to their feet and shoved them towards their dune buggy. 'All right. Take us to her.'

'It's irremediable,' Spike said in a quivering voice. 'Koopa won't let us back in without her little meteorite piece.'

'Wait,' Luigi said. 'You mean that stone she wore?'

'Yes,' said Iggy. 'It chipped off the big meteorite sixty-five million years ago, causing a harmonic divergence between your dimension and ours. When it's put back into place, the dimensions will reunite.'

'Then Koopa can invade your world,' Spike said. 'The mammals will be overrun by goombas.'

'I don't get it,' Mario said. 'Why doesn't he just come through like you clowns did?'

'The gateway?' Iggy shook his head. 'Too dangerous, too small . . . And it was sealed for years until something on your side must have blasted it open again.'

'Scapelli!' Mario gasped.

'Look,' Luigi said impatiently. 'We gotta find this meteorite piece and save Daisy.'

'And you two guys are gonna help us,' Mario told the ex-goons.

Iggy and Spike gave each other questioning looks.

'With our new, evolutionarily enhanced brains, it does seem like the correct course of action,' said Iggy.

Luigi remembered something. 'Mario, we gotta find that spiky chick in the red. By that bar, remember?'

'A big spiky red babe?' Spike asked.

Mario and Luigi nodded.

'Bertha from the Boom Boom Bar,' said Iggy, glancing back at the smashed dune buggy. 'Now, if only Spikeasauralopolus hadn't destroyed our vehicle.'

'Ah, but I have an idea,' said Spike, raising a thin bony finger. 'Snifits have sludge-gulpers.'

'Who have what?' Luigi asked.

'You'll see,' said Iggy.

It was night-time before they reached the vast refuse dumps that surrounded Dinohattan. Giant floodlights lit mountains of rubbish and filth. Sludge-gulpers, huge trucks filled with refuse, dumped fresh loads. Men driving bulldozers pushed the rubbish into mountains. The drivers and other workers wore gas masks and jump-suits with Snifit stencilled on their backs.

Holding their noses, Mario and Luigi sneaked up to the two closest Snifits. Mario took out his spanner and clubbed one over the head. The other Snifit turned to see what had happened.

'Do it!' Mario shouted at his brother. But when Luigi reached down to his tool belt for a spanner, his jaw dropped. His belt was there but –

'I lost all my tools!' he gasped.

Clunk! Mario had to smack the other Snifit on the head. A moment later, dressed as Snifits, with their faces hidden under the gas masks, Mario and Luigi drove an empty sludge-gulper towards the city-dump checkpoint. Iggy and Spike hid on the floor.

'I can't believe you lost all your tools!' Mario ranted. 'Do you know the value of that tool set I bought you?'

'I thought it was a starter set.'

'OK, sure, but still,' Mario sulked.

'Shh!' Luigi raised a finger to the nose of his gas mask. 'Calm down. We're coming to the checkpoint.'

They reached a barred gate where guards in gas masks stood. Mario and Luigi nodded at them. The guards nodded back and lifted the gate. Mario steered the sludge-gulper through the checkpoint, and they joined a convoy of trucks heading back through the night towards the city.

On the way they passed a huge greenish statue of a woman wearing a spiked crown and holding one hand high above her head. Mario and Luigi pulled off their gas masks and stared at it.

'What's that?' Mario asked. 'It looks almost familiar.'

'The Statue of Repression,' Iggy said. 'It's Koopa's droll paean to his neofascist monarchy.'

'Koopa the Self-referential, as it were,' Spike added with a smirk.

'What is all this Koopa-the-blank stuff?' Luigi asked. 'We've seen posters for Koopa the Sportsman, Koopa the Cruel, Koopa the Stud. Doesn't anybody run against this guy?'

'Koopa the Sensitive ran four years ago,' Spike said. 'He got only two per cent of the vote.'

'If he's so unpopular, can't someone run against him?' Luigi asked.

'Not possible,' said Iggy.

'So you can elect anyone, so long as it's Koopa?' Mario guessed.

'Precisely,' said Spike.

'What kind of system is that?' Luigi asked.

'Democracy,' said Iggy.

'What was it like before Koopa?' Mario asked.

'Oh, it was lovely,' Iggy sighed. 'Under the velvet glove of our philosopher King Bowser. Water flowed. We were free.'

'Then why do you put up with this now?' Luigi asked, gesturing towards the crumbling, fungus-covered city they had just entered.

'Actually, we never really thought about it,' Spike said.

'Come to think of it,' Iggy said, 'it has become a rather cruel, oppressive place, hasn't it?'

Mario parked the sludge-gulper in front of the Boom Boom Bar, and they went in. Lights flashed and super-loud music pounded their eardrums as they watched the crowd dance.

'Check your belts, gentlemen,' Iggy said, gesturing to the cloakroom near the entrance to the bar. Mario and Luigi handed over their tool belts and stepped into the crowd. They soon spotted Bertha on the dance floor, grinding and writhing. Around her neck was the leather thong with the meteorite piece.

'Change the world, my boys,' Spike said, patting

the brothers on the shoulders. 'Meanwhile, Iggy and I will retire to the bar for a drink.'

Back inside the cloakroom, the attendant stared at a wanted poster of Mario and Luigi pinned to the wall. She lifted the phone. 'Did I hear there was a reward being offered for some plumbers?' she whispered into the receiver. 'I think you'll find them at the Boom Boom Bar.'

Luigi and Mario huddled in the crowd, watching Bertha dance.

'I'll take care of her,' Mario whispered. 'No woman can resist the charms of a Mario.'

A second later he sauntered through the rough crowd towards the big woman in red. As he got close, he did a couple of quick, slick dance moves designed to catch Bertha's eye.

'Hi, the name's Mario,' he said with a smile. 'I'm your main man, your ram-a-dam, your can o' Spam.'

Pow! Bertha slugged him so hard in the jaw that he flew backwards across the floor and landed at his brother's feet.

'Her can o' Spam?' Luigi asked sceptically as he helped Mario to his feet.

'Maybe I have to try a different approach,' Mario said with a shrug, and started across the floor again. When Bertha saw him coming, she made another fist and drew her hand back.

'Please,' Mario begged. 'Hit me again. I've never seen such fluidity of form or such grace. The way your lip curled in that sensual snarl as you rocked your fist back. The way your knuckles tenderly crunched when you brought them smashing into my face.'

The band started to play a low song. Bertha smiled.

'Dance with me, and I'll hit you all you want,' she murmured, putting her arms around him. Mario swallowed hard and began to dance with her. He had to find some way to get the meteorite piece from around her neck. As they swayed back and forth, Mario moved his lips towards her throat. He managed to close his teeth around the meteorite piece. A moment later he spun her around, and the thong came off her neck. Bertha didn't notice.

The song ended, and Mario quickly headed back towards Luigi. Iggy and Spike had got drunk and were now standing on the bar, doing an anti-Koopa rap song. Mario nudged his brother.

'Look what I got,' he whispered, handing him the meteorite piece.

Luigi took the rock and pointed at the door. 'We also got trouble.'

Mario turned to look. Lena was standing in the doorway with a bunch of boombas.

'Time to disappear,' Luigi whispered. As he and his brother tried to mix with the dancers, the goombas pushed through the crowd and grabbed Iggy and Spike.

The band started playing a new song, and the crowd around Luigi and Mario began to do the Dactyl, a dance with a lot of steps the brothers didn't know. Despite their attempts to hide behind the other dancers, Lena quickly spotted them.

'There they are!' she cried. 'Get them!'

The goombas soon had Luigi cornered. He tossed the meteorite piece to Mario, but it fell short. Mario dived across the dance floor to catch it.

A split second later, Lena's spiked heel came down on his hand. Mario gasped in pain and looked up at the red-haired woman.

'Nice catch, plumber,' Lena said, snatching the thong from his hand. Now that she had the meteorite piece, the goombas who'd cornered Luigi backed off. Luigi gave Mario a nod and the two brothers ran for the door.

'Don't let them go, you idiots!' Lena shouted at the goombas, who immediately gave chase.

The brothers had to get out of the Boom Boom Bar fast. Mario was in the lead, pushing through the crowd. The exit door was only a few feet ahead . . .

Then Bertha stepped into his path. Mario stared up at her and recognized the look in her eyes. It wasn't anger. It wasn't revenge. It was love. She opened her arms and grabbed him.

'Sorry, Bertha,' Mario gasped, trying to squirm out of her arms before the goombas got there. 'This isn't the time . . .'

But Bertha wasn't concerned about the goombas. She had eyes only for Mario. As she pulled him closer, he was certain she was going to kiss him with her giant red lips, but at the last second she pressed them to his ear.

'I now how you can get out of here,' she whispered.

'Really?' Mario gasped. 'Do I have to kiss you?'

'Nope.'

Mario was so overjoyed he kissed Bertha anyway. Beaming, Bertha pulled out of the kiss, spun around, and slugged the cloakroom attendant. Mario and Luigi followed Bertha into the cloakroom and quickly strapped their tool belts back on.

'Here,' Bertha said, grabbing two pairs of thwomp stompers from the shelf. 'Use these.'

She tossed them the stompers, then span around and smashed her fist into the face of a goomba trying to get into the cloakroom. The brothers started to pull the boots on.

'How do these work?' Mario asked as he closed the buckles.

'Easy, Mario,' Luigi said. 'Just stomp 'em.'

'Oh, of course!' Mario rolled his eyes. 'How stupid of me not to know.'

A moment later the thwomp stompers were securely fastened to their feet. More goombas were trying to force their way into the cloakroom. Bertha was straining to keep them out.

'How can we thank you for helping us?' Luigi asked her as she held off five of the giant reptilian creatures.

'Stop Koopa's evil reign,' Bertha said through clenched teeth. Suddenly she slipped, and the goombas charged into the cloakroom. Mario and Luigi stomped down and immediately blasted upwards through the skylight, sending a thousand splinters of glass raining down on the glowering goombas below.

The brothers landed on the disco's roof. On the street below they could see more goombas arriving. Suddenly Luigi saw a small black wind-up bomb fall out of the fungus near him.

'Hey, Mario,' he said, tugging on this brother's shirt. 'Look, another one.'

'Not now!' Mario yelled.

'Have you ever noticed how these things always appear out of the fungus when we're in trouble?'

Luigi asked.

But Mario wasn't interested. 'Come on,' he shouted, 'this way!'

They jumped off the roof into the back of a passing sludge-gulper and sank up to their neck in foul-smelling rubbish.

'Boy, this stuff stinks,' Luigi gasped as he caught his breath.

'At least we're free,' Mario replied.

'Maybe, but Lena's back in the tower with the meteorite piece by now,' Luigi said hopelessly. 'It's impossible to get in there.'

'Nothing's impossible,' Mario corrected him. 'Unlikely, maybe. Even improbable. But not impossible.'

'Then let's do it,' Luigi said through clenched teeth.

High in the tower, Koopa entered a room where a large bulb of yellowish fungus hung from a fungus-enveloped de-evolution cone.

'My, my.' Koopa shook his head as he spoke to the cone. 'You *have* let yourself go. See, I'm not such a bad guy. You always said you wanted to be everywhere. So I granted your wish. But you know what? You can try to choke this little dimension as much as you want, because I'm out of here. I'm headed for the big world. I got plumbers coming with the rest of the meteorite. Soon-to-be-dead plumbers.'

Koopa paused and stared at the throne beneath the fungus. 'By the way, I don't care what you think of me, Bowser. I'll never mix with a mammal. Never! I believe in purity of lizarddom. Pretty soon we'll be back on top.'

Many storeys below, at the base of the tower, a sludge-gulper pulled up to a loading dock. Mario and Luigi jumped out. They quickly peeled off their rubbish-stained clothes and pulled on clean outfits they found hanging near the door to the tower. Mario's was red with blue arms and pockets, and a red cap. Luigi's was green with blue arms and pockets, and a green cap.

'Not bad,' Luigi said. 'Maybe we'll get to keep these.'

Mario carefully buckled on his tool belt.

'Treat your tools like a friend,' Mario lectured his brother. 'That way they'll always be on your side.'

'Hey, Mario,' Luigi said. 'How is it that for every possible situation, you got a saying about tools?'

'They all come from Poppa,' Mario said reverently. 'And he got 'em from Grandpoppa.'

The brothers went through a door and found themselves in a boiler room. The walls were lined with rusty girders and yellow fungus. Steam hissed, and a furnace beneath a boiler roared. Against one wall was the door to an elevator. Mario took a step towards it.

'We can't just go take the lift,' Luigi said.

'Obviously we can't take the lift,' Mario replied. 'What do you think I am, some kind of idiot?'

'So how are we gonna get upstairs?' Luigi asked.

'Like a Mario would,' his brother said, staring

at the boiler and the huge vent pipes lining the walls. 'Ingeniously . . . Luigi, remove that outlet valve from the boiler body. I'm gonna freeze the building so we'll have a way to get down.'

Suddenly an alarm above the door started to ring, and lights began to flash. Luigi quickly got to work on the outlet valve. 'I understand you working out a way to get down, Mario,' said Luigi in a slightly panicked voice. 'But I still don't understand how we're gonna get up.'

Mario thought quickly. 'There's only one possible way,' he said, walking to the lift and pushing the UP button.

'The lift,' Luigi said with a nod. 'Gee, Mario, that sure is ingenious.'

The lift doors opened, and Mario and Luigi got in. Alarms were still ringing, lights were still flashing. The doors opened and the lift began to rise. Mario and Luigi stared up at the brightly lit numbers above the lift doors.

'We just better pray no one gets —' Mario began to say. Suddenly they hard a *ding* and the lift stopped. As the doors began to open, Mario and Luigi quickly span around and faced the back of the lift. They heard someone step in behind them and press a button. The doors began to close. Mario and Luigi glanced at each other, then slowly looked around. Two goombas had got in.

They must have been in such a rush that they didn't even give the brothers a good look. Now they stood staring up at the numbers above the doors.

Ding! The lift stopped again. Mario and Luigi stared wide-eyed at each other as the doors began to open. They quickly jumped behind the first two goombas and hid as more goombas entered the lift.

Ding! Once again the lift stopped and the doors opened. Even more goombas entered. Mario and Luigi managed to slide unnoticed behind them. They stared at each other in disbelief. At this rate, it was going to be a long trip to the top.

At the sound of the alarm, Koopa strode quickly out of the fungus room. Lena was coming towards him in the corridor, followed by several goombas carrying Spike and Iggy.

'You'll be interested to know that these two were at the Boom Boom Bar, preaching your overthrow,' Lena informed him.

'Really?' Koopa stared at his ex-goons. 'I'm very disappointed in you two.'

'Fascist.' Spike spat the word out distastefully.

'Oppressor of the proletariat!' Iggy said.

Koopa waved them away and started down the corridor again. Lena hurried behind him.

'Wait! I have something else for you,' she said.

'Not now,' Koopa yelled. 'I have saboteurs in the tower. I still have no meteorite piece and I'm about to lose everything.'

'But this is important,' Lena insisted. 'We have to talk.'

'Does it have to do with you?' Koopa asked without breaking his stride. 'Does it have to do with us?'

'Yes, most definitely,' Lena said.

'Then type up a memo and submit it through the proper channels,' Koopa snapped and stormed off, leaving an angry Lena alone in the hallway.

Lena looked down at the meteorite piece in her fist. 'No,' she muttered to herself. 'I won't submit it through the proper channels. If I want to get something done around here, I'll do it myself.'

She quickly turned and stalked off towards Koopa's suite. Throwing open he door, she found Princess Daisy talking to the goomba who had once been Toad the street musician. The goomba was carrying a tray with a steak on it.

'Sorry, but I'm a vegetarian,' Daisy was saying. 'I don't eat anything with a face. And I hope you realize I'm being held against my will. It's a flagrant violation of my civil liberties.'

'Get out!' Lena shouted at the goomba, who

quickly left. Lena turned to face Daisy. In the corner, restrained by a metal chain, Yoshi growled at her.

'Hello ... and goodbye,' Daisy said, turning her back on Lena. Yoshi growled again.

'Loyal to the royal family through and through,' Lena muttered, pulling a long needle out of her dress and coming up behind Daisy. 'Fine. Everyone should have a right to what's theirs ... except when *I* want it instead!'

Lena lunged at Daisy with the needle, but Yoshi's long tongue went around her ankle and tripped her. The little dinosaur began dragging Lena towards him.

'Get him off me!' Lena cried.

Daisy hesitated for a moment, but then saw the opportunity to escape and dashed out into a hallway. Unfortunately, several goombas saw her and gave chase. Daisy began to run. She went around a corner and skidded to a halt. More goombas were coming towards her, carrying Iggy and Spike. Daisy was trapped.

'You miserable low-lifes!' she shouted at Koopa's former goons.

'You're right,' Spike replied. 'We are miserable low-lifes.'

'But don't all of God's creatures find themselves in a similar lot?' Iggy argued.

'Huh?' Daisy frowned, but the goombas chasing

her were closing in from behind. Suddenly the goomba who had been Toad stepped among them, carrying a large tray of vegetables. In the confusion, Daisy doubled back, ducking under the goombas' outstretched arms. They tried to follow her, but Toad the goomba blocked their path.

'Ha!' Spike laughed. 'A goomba with a sense of tradition!'

'Extradition!' Iggy shouted. 'Put us down, churls.'

'Tell them to put us down, princess,' Spike called.

Iggy and Spike wriggled out of the goombas' grasp and followed Daisy down the corridor.

'Princess Daisy,' Iggy gasped. 'We are your loyal supporters.'

'We've been on your father's side since his demise,' Spike added, glancing at Iggy. 'Well, at least *I* have . . .'

The three of them ducked through a doorway and found themselves in the fungus room. Daisy stared uncomfortably at the yellow bulb of fungus perched above the throne.

'I realize the following may be something of a shock to you,' Spike said. 'But Princess Daisy, may I present your father.'

'Our patriarch,' Iggy added. 'King Bowser.'

Daisy stared in utter disbelief. All around them

alarms were ringing and lights were flashing. Spike and Iggy glanced nervously at each other.

'Uh, perhaps at such a delicate moment, a retreat is in order.' Spike suggested, backing nervously towards the door.

'He who fights and runs away, lives to fight another day,' Iggy added.

They dashed out of the door. Daisy hardly noticed. She was fascinated by the fungus. It was moving and almost seemed to point at something. Daisy looked towards the door and saw Koopa's pet dinosaur.

'Yoshi,' Daisy gasped.

The little Tyrannosaurus rex was beckoning her towards a console covered with buttons and security monitors. One of the monitors showed Luigi and Mario crawling through some sort of shaft. Daisy frantically pushed the buttons on the console, trying to call to them.

To escape the goombas in the lift, Mario and Luigi had crawled out through the hatch in the roof and into a ventilation shaft. Suddenly Daisy's voice echoed towards them. 'Luigi! Mario! Can you hear me?'

'It's her!' Luigi cried. 'Yes, we hear you! We're coming!'

Once again Daisy's voice echoed through the shaft. 'I'm in the de-evolution chamber!'

Mario and Luigi followed her voice, but the ventilation shaft suddenly ended. Luigi crawled to the edge and looked down into an endless black chasm.

'Now what are we gonna do?' Mario asked.

Luigi thought for a moment. 'Jump to the other side.

'What other side?' Mario asked.

'I can make it,' Luigi insisted. 'I got a good feeling.

'How do you know?' Mario gasped, as his brother crouched down at the edge of the shaft. 'Don't do it! You'll fall! Luigi, no!'

Luigi sprang across the dark chasm. Suddenly he stopped in mid-air and just hung there.

'Hey, look, Mario!' he shouted. 'I told you it would work. Come on, give it a shot. You just gotta have faith!'

As Mario crouched down to jump, Luigi felt something tugging at the collar of his overalls. Felling it with his fingers, he realized he'd become caught on a winch hook. *That* was why he was hanging in mid-air.

'Wait, Mario!' he yelled. 'It's not faith. It's just a hook!'

Too late. Mario leapt towards him. Their eyes met for a second, then Mario plummeted down into the dark chasm.

'Ahhhhhhhhhhh!' Mario screamed. Luigi cringed in horror. Suddenly he heard a loud *sproing!* The next thing Luigi knew, Mario bounced back up in the air, swinging his fists wildly at him.

'There's a piece of fungus stretched −' Mario started to say, then disappeared again. *Sproing!* He bounced up again.

'Across the duct,' he continued. 'I'm alive, but −' He disappeared again. *Sproing!* He bounced up again.

'But I'm gonna kill you!' he shouted. He grabbed Luigi's outstretched hands. The two brothers hung over the dark chasm.

'You don't mean that,' Luigi said.

'I do,' Mario insisted. 'I'm telling you. If we die here, I'm gonna kill you so bad you're gonna wish you were dead. Now, are you gonna save your loving brother or what?'

As Luigi held on to his brother, a strange look appeared in his eyes. 'Hey, Mario, there's something I've been thinking about.'

'And you want to tell me *now*?' Mario asked incredulously as he stared down into the endless, inky darkness below.

'Yeah,' Luigi said. 'I just thought you should know that I *do* have family pride.'

'What?'

'Remember back at our apartment, before we

went to Bella Napoli for dinner?' Luigi asked. 'You said I had no pride in being a Mario. Well, I do. I'm real proud to be a Mario, Mario. And I'm real proud to be your brother.'

'I'm touched,' Mario replied. 'I'd hug you, but then you'd be an only child.'

'No, seriously,' Luigi insisted. 'I mean it.'

Suddenly Daisy's voice echoed again into the shaft. 'Come *on*, Luigi!'

'Right, right,' Luigi shouted back. 'I'm coming!'

Luigi started to swing himself and Mario back and forth over the chasm. Suddenly, at the top of an upswing, the hook ripped out of Luigi's overalls. The brothers flew through the air and landed in a heap at the entrance to another shaft.

'Come on,' Luigi shouted, scrambling to his feet. 'We've got a girl to save.'

Not far away, Koopa was walking quickly through a hallway. Simon approached him. 'Good news, sir,' the police officer said. 'The troops are in place, ready to de-evolve the mammals.'

Koopa stopped and stared at him. 'In place? Ready to do what? Who ordered their deployment?'

'You did, sir,' Simon replied. 'Lena relayed your command. We carried it out immediately.'

95

Koopa's eyes narrowed with fury. So Lena had the meteorite piece and had decided to act on her own . . .

Mario and Luigi pushed through a wall grate and came out into a corridor near the fungus room. Brandishing tools and ready for a fight, they pushed through the door, but inside they found Daisy alone. She and Luigi rushed into each other's arms and embraced.

'You OK?' Luigi asked.

'Yes.'

'I hope coming to save you isn't too forward of me or anything,' Luigi said apologetically.

'No,' Daisy said, gazing up at him. 'I just can't believe you're here. I mean, it's hard to believe any of this, but you've gone so far out of your way.'

'Well, it's true I'm not the kind of guy who usually chases girls,' Luigi said. 'At least, not into other dimensions.'

Daisy smiled and hugged him again. Their faces moved closer, and they were about to kiss when a strand of fungus suddenly dropped between them.

'Dad!' Daisy scolded her father. The fungus quickly rose back to the ceiling. Luigi turned and looked quizzically at Daisy.

'Uh, this may sound kind of weird,' Daisy stammered. 'I mean, I know it's a little early in our relationship, but, er, Luigi, I'd like you to meet my father.'

Lugi stared at the blob of fungus.

'At least, he *was* my father,' Daisy explained. 'He used to be the king here until Koopa turned him into this.'

Luigi reached forward, took some fungus in his hand and shook it. 'It's an honour, sir. And I especially want to thank you for all your help.'

'Next you'll be singing to mildew in the shower,' Mario muttered.

'Mario, think about it,' Luigi said. 'This fungus has been helping us all along. Remember the car? And the shaft? He *wants* us to help defeat Koopa.' Luigi turned to the fungus. 'Don't worry, sir. We'll have your daughter safely back in no time.'

Meanwhile, Daisy turned to Mario. 'Is Daniella safe?'

'Daniella?' Mario slapped himself in the forehead for forgetting her. 'Oh, man, is she gonna be mad. I was supposed to take her to the roller derby.'

'You mean, you don't know?' Daisy gasped.

'Know what?' Mario asked.

'Daniella's *here*,' Daisy said. 'She's downstairs, in the women's detention room.'

'Here?' Mario's eyes widened. He burst out of the room and back into the hall. 'Daniella! I'm coming for you, baby!'

Luigi and Daisy raced out behind him.

'Daniella?' Mario cried again.

'Yes?' A voice answered. But it was a male voice. Mario and the others turned around and found Koopa coming towards them with his goombas.

'Oops, I'm sorry,' Koopa said. 'I bet you meant the other Daniella. The unneeded one. The one wasting precious space and air.'

The goombas quickly grabbed Luigi and Daisy. But Mario was still free. Now he had to choose between saving his brother or saving his girlfriend.

'Go, Mario!' Luigi shouted at him. 'Go get Daniella!'

'But . . .' Mario hesitated.

'Just go!' Luigi urged him.

'OK, but I'll be back for you!' Mario shouted as he started to run. 'I swear it!'

'Get him!' Koopa shouted at his goombas. 'And ready the troops. We're going down!'

As Mario ran down the hall, he couldn't help looking back at his brother. Despite his promise, he knew this might be the last time he ever saw Luigi. Luigi waved and Mario nodded. A second later he turned the corner into a new hallway . . .

A burst of fireballs almost got him. Mario quickly span around and headed in a new direction, followed by armed goombas. Where was that detention room? he wondered. Suddenly he heard female voices.

'Hey, you goombas!' A familiar voice shouted. 'We're getting sick of it down here.'

'Yeah,' said another. 'If you don't let us out, my brother Jimmy's gonna be all over you like white on rice.'

Mario smiled. He'd know those voices anywhere. They were girls from Brooklyn! He quickly pushed through a door and found himself on a platform. Down below, Daniella and four other girls were yelling at a goomba. Mario waved, trying to get Daniella's attention. Finally Daniella noticed him. Mario motioned to her to very quietly let the other girls know he was there. But just then Angelica saw him and shrieked, 'Get down here and save our butts!'

The other girls started shouting, too. 'Thank God! Hurry!'

The goomba span around and raised his weapon. Mario grabbed a hanging light and swung off the platform like Tarzan, knocking the goomba flat on his back. Daniella leapt into Mario's arms and kissed him.

'Didn't I tell you my Mario would be here?' she asked the other girls.

'That's right,' Mario said. 'I came all this way with only one thing on my mind. Rescuing you . . . er, all of you. You're all the girls missing from Brooklyn, right?'

'Well, Angie's from Queens,' Daniella said, 'but she's OK.'

'Except I'm freezing my butt off,' Angelica complained, pointing at the wall. 'There's cold air blowin' in from that duct over there.'

'That's correct, sweetheart,' Mario said proudly. 'And that's exactly where we're headed.' He started to herd the girls towards the ventilation shaft. Suddenly the door on the other side of the room burst open, and a dozen armed goombas rushed in, firing fireballs and acid guns.

'Grab that mattress!' Mario shouted. Two of the girls ran to a nearby bed and took the mattress off it. They turned and rushed back towards Mario and the others, but the goombas were almost there . . .

From high in his tower, Koopa peered down at Koopa Square, where thousands of goombas were grouping for the invasion of the mammal world.

Koopa turned back to his generals, who were standing to attention in his suite. Several goombas held Daisy and Luigi captive to one side.

'Are all special teams ready?' Koopa asked.

'Yes, sir,' one of his generals replied. 'Goombas are merging in areas two, four, five, and seven. All three thousand are ready to go.'

The door to the suite burst open and Simon rushed in, followed by two goombas escorting a semi-conscious Lena.

'Sir,' Simon said, holding out his hand. 'I believe you were looking for this.'

He opened his hand. In his palm was the meteorite piece on the leather thong. With a broad smile, Koopa took it.

'Very good work,' he said. 'It's funny, isn't it? How days that start out so bad can end up so good.'

Koopa turned towards the goombas holding Luigi and Daisy. 'I guess I'm not a good guy,' he said to Daisy. 'But I am going to give you the chance to fulfil your special destiny. *You* can fit this meteorite piece back into the meteor.' He snapped his finger. 'Then it'll be goodbye sub-dimension. Don't you just love moving house?'

13

Thanks to Mario's earlier sabotage, the inside of the ventilation duct was lined with ice. With a *whoosh!* the mattress shot downwards. Mario and the Brooklyn girls held on tight.

'Last exit to Brooklyn!' Mario shouted as they corkscrewed through the shaft, ducking huge hanging icicles.

Then Mario saw the bottomless chasm ahead.

'Lean!' he cried.

Shrieking, the girls all leaned. The mattress banked up along one side of the shaft and just missed the chasm.

'Yaaa-hooo!' they screamed.

Crash! The mattress smashed through a grating and into Koopa Square. Still holding on tight, Mario and the girls knocked over pedestrians and cyclists. Ahead, Mario spotted Koopa and his goombas leading the handcuffed Daisy and Luigi into the subway tunnel.

'Devo guns ready?' Koopa shouted as they neared the tunnel entrance. 'Come on, let's go!'

'Yaaaaa!' Mario bellowed as the mattress ploughed into the crowd, knocking over Koopa. Half a dozen goombas crashed through the window of the thwomp stomper store, sending thwomp stompers flying all over the pavement.

Luigi rushed towards his brother. 'Mario, you're amazing! Are you OK?'

Mario was flushed with excitement, but he just shrugged.

They turned to see Koopa rising to his feet with a fireball gun in his hands. 'Too late, humans. Looks like I win. Next time I see you, you and all your fellow humans from the other dimension will be de-evolved into . . . wait, don't tell me. Uh, not puppies. Not bunnies. Monkeys! That's it!'

'Mario,' Luigi whispered, nodding at the scattered thwomp stompers. 'The boots!'

Mario grabbed a thwomp stomper and launched it at Koopa, knocking him backwards and out of sight. Then he launched another boot, sending a food stall smashing into the goombas. Some of the goombas ran. Others were trapped under the overturned stall. A moment later everything went quiet.

Ker-blam! A fireball nearly blew them away. Koopa had climbed into the huge metal bucket above the square. He clenched the meteor piece in his teeth as he took aim again.

'Hey, Mario!' Luigi yelled, still struggling with his handcuffs. 'Get us out of these cuffs.'

'Here, take my belt,' Mario said, unhitching his tool belt and tossing it to Daniella. 'Help them get out of those cuffs. I'll get the rock off the lizard.'

'Here, Mario,' Luigi shouted. 'Take my belt.'

'But it's empty,' Mario said.

'Trust the fungus,' Luigi said. Daniella freed him from his handcuffs, and he tossed the belt to Mario. Inside one of the pockets, Mario found a mushroom and a round, small bomb.

'Don't forget!' Luigi shouted. 'The fungus is among us!'

Mario hitched on the belt, then climbed up a fungus vine and swung towards Koopa. But the lizard king fired a fireball, severing the fungus in two.

'Only a miracle's gonna save you, plumber!' Koopa shouted as Mario started to fall.

But Mario managed to grab a rail beneath the bucket. As Koopa searched the square below for him, Mario silently pulled himself up behind. *Wham!* He smashed Koopa in the back of the head, sending the meteorite piece flying.

Down, down it fell towards . . . Lena, who was

running through the streets below. Seeing the meteorite piece fall, she vaulted over a railing and caught it, but a moment later she fell on to a power grid.

Psssssstt! Lena's red hair ballooned as she was electrified. Mario was sure she'd been fried for good, but amazingly she jumped up and ran down into the subway entrance.

'We've got to stop her!' Daisy shouted. 'Before she gets to the meteorite!'

'Let's go, girls!' Luigi yelled, and ran into the subway tunnel after Lena.

Unaware that Lena now had the meteorite piece, Koopa frantically searched the floor of the bucket. Mario knew he had to stall Koopa to give Luigi and Daisy time to escape. Untying the leather shoelace of his work boot, Mario held it out towards Koopa, pretending he had the rock inside his hand.

'Is this what you're looking for?' he asked.

'Give me that rock,' Koopa growled.

Mario leapt out of the bucket and into the traffic below. Koopa instantly followed, chasing him through the traffic and up on to an empty walkway. Once again Mario held out the leather lace.

'Come and get it, lizard-breath,' he taunted.

As Koopa stepped towards him, wisps of flame

licked out of the end of his fireball gun. Mario searched desperately for something to defend himself with. He plunged his hand into Luigi's empty tool belt and pulled out the little bomb. He had no idea what it was, but when Koopa saw it, he froze.

'Stop!' he gasped. 'Put that down!'

So it is dangerous, Mario thought. He quickly wound up the bomb and set it down. Koopa stared in terror as it began to roll towards him. But then suddenly, the bomb slipped through the grating on to the street below.

Mario and Koopa both gritted their teeth, waiting for a tremendous explosion ... But nothing happened. Koopa smiled and started towards Mario again. He was only a few feet away now. The nozzle of the fireball gun was so close that Mario could see the pilot-light and feel its evil heat.

Koopa started to pull the trigger. Mario knew he'd be fried to a crisp if he didn't do something fast. He grabbed the barrel of the fireball gun and ... blew out the pilot-light. A second later, Koopa pulled the trigger. *Click ... click ...* With the pilot-light out, nothing happened.

Down in the subway tunnel, Lena entered the huge underground meteor chamber. At its centre was the rounded, silvery top of the giant meteor, glowing at its edges. Just as she climbed on to the meteor, Luigi, Daisy, and the Brooklyn girls burst in.

'You're too late!' Lena cackled as she thrust the meteorite piece into place. 'It's mine! I've earned the power!'

But the power was too much for her. As Luigi and the others watched, a giant crackling wave of energy burst out of the meteor and enveloped Lena. It was only a second before she disintegrated. As the bright light faded, they saw her elongated outline etched into the chamber wall like a fossil.

The rock wall began to swirl. Flashes of energy crashed like thunder.

'What's happening?' Daisy gasped.

'It's the gateway!' Luigi shouted.

'Yeah,' Daniella said. 'That's where we came through.'

'Hurry!' Luigi shouted. 'And be careful on the other side. Just . . . uh . . . don't look down!'

Angelica stepped towards the swirling rock, then hesitated.

'Go,' Luigi shouted. 'It's shrinking.'

Angelica took a deep breath and flung herself at the wall, disappearing into the swirling liquid rock.

Another girl dived through. Then it was Daniella's turn. At the last second she turned to Luigi.

'Tell Mario . . .' she began, wishing she could protect her boyfriend somehow. Then she shook her head. 'Forget it. He never listens to anything.'

Daniella went through the wall. That was all the Brooklyn girls except Daisy. Where was she? Luigi looked around and saw her climbing the meteor. The meteorite piece vibrated as it was slowly being sucked into the meteor.

'Daisy, don't!' Luigi shouted.

Ignoring him, she grabbed the meteorite piece. Luigi knew she was trying to stop the invasion by preventing the two dimensions from merging. Now he heard a loud reverberating sound and saw waves of energy skittering across the tunnel walls. Luigi stared up at Lena's imprint on the wall, terrified that Daisy's imprint would soon be there as well.

In Koopa Square, Koopa and Mario heard the reverberating sound, too. Everything around them began to shimmer and grow translucent.

'It's happening!' Koopa gasped, glaring at Mario. 'You don't have the meteorite piece at all, you filthy mammal!' He turned and looked around frantically. 'The invasion! Where are my goombas?'

A large group of goombas was standing near the subway tunnel, but as Mario and Koopa watched, they began to shimmer out of existence. Near them on the street, cars began to disappear. Mario looked down at himself. Now he, too, was starting to disappear.

14

Back at the Scapelli excavation site in Brooklyn, Daniella and the other Brooklyn girls had already called the newspapers. Now they were surrounded by newspaper reporters and radio and TV crews from all the major stations. Even a van from *Our Miraculous World* showed up.

'You say you were kidnapped and taken to a dinosaur world?' a sceptical reporter asked.

'That's correct,' Angelica said.

'And you were rescued by plumbers?' asked a reporter, his voice growing even more incredulous.

'Not just any plumbers,' Daniella informed him. 'The Mario brothers.'

Nearby, Anthony Scapelli shook his head and turned to one of his associates. 'Those guys will do anything for publicity.'

The reporters and TV crews were shaking their heads, too. 'Let's go,' one irritated reporter said. 'We're wasting our time here.'

They turned back to their vans – and came face-to-face with a group of bewildered goombas who'd just materialized.

'What the . . .?' shouted a confused reporter.

The air around them began to shimmer.

'Look!' Daniella shouted, pointing across the river to Manhattan, where the World Trade Center was slowly turning into Koopa's towers. Then suddenly Koopa and Mario materialized in the air over the excavation pit and fell with a thud. At the sight of the goombas, the other TV crews had scattered. Only the guys from *Our Miraculous World* were getting it all on tape.

'That's him!' the Brooklyn girls shouted, pointing at Mario. 'He's the guy who rescued us! Hey, Mario!'

Daniella rushed towards Mario, but she wasn't alone. Anthony Scapelli was right behind her. There was no way he was going to let Mario get all this free publicity.

Meanwhile Koopa looked around, delighted. Finally! The mammal world was his! He grabbed a devo gun from a nearby goomba.

'Welcome to my world!' he shouted with glee as his finger closed around the trigger. 'And goodbye!'

Koopa fired at Mario, who managed to duck out of the way. The blast hit Scapelli, who was instantly transformed into a chimpanzee in a fancy suit.

Mario reached into his tool belt and pulled out the mushroom. 'Trust the fungus!' he shouted.

Koopa fired at him again, but the mushroom absorbed the beam and de-evolved into a giant, more primitive mushroom. Mario threw it like a Frisbee, knocking Koopa's devo gun into the excavation pit. A second later, Mario and the lizard king rolled to the ground, locked in mortal hand-to-hand combat.

Back in the meteor chamber, Luigi was rigging a makeshift lever to pull the meteorite piece back out. Using Mario's tools, he attached a wheel-puller to the meteorite piece, extended it with a small pipe, and then added a large wrench for leverage. Sweating and straining, he and Daisy pulled as hard as they could. The reverberating noise grew louder.

'It's working!' Daisy shouted.

With a final desperate tug, the meteorite piece popped out of the meteor. Daisy grabbed it. 'Come on!' she shouted.

Mario and Koopa were wrestling for the devo gun when they suddenly shimmered away again, this time reappearing in Koopa Square, along with the goombas.

'Don't just stand there, you pea-brained morons!' Koopa screamed at them.

But instead of coming to his aid, the goombas began – most unexpectedly – to dance. His face contorting with anger, Koopa looked around and saw the goomba who was once Toad playing a harmonica. The lizard king filled with fury, and as he did so, he began to regress. Within moments he was half man, half Tyrannosaurus rex. He grabbed another goomba's gun and aimed it at Mario. This time he wasn't going to miss!

But the forgotten bomb had begun to fizzle beneath them.

Ka-blamm! The bomb exploded. Koopa was blown into the air and landed back in the bucket. He struggled to his feet and once again aimed his weapon at Mario.

'Mario!' Luigi shouted as he and Daisy burst out of the subway tunnel. Luigi grabbed a devo gun from a dancing goomba and threw it to Mario, who span around and fired the gun at Koopa.

'See ya later, alligator!' Mario shouted triumphantly as the devo beam hit Koopa, knocking him backwards into the bucket.

Suddenly there was silence. Mario and the

others crept cautiously towards the bucket. Had they made Koopa into goop?

They were only a few feet away when a giant Tyrannosaurus rex leapt up, snapping its mammoth jaws and almost taking Mario's head off.

Terrified, Mario and the others leaped back and grabbed devo guns.

Fwooooom! Firing all at once, the devo beams converged and the terrible dinosaur began to shrink. Teetering on the edge of the bucket, it lost its grip and began to fall. It was de-evolving into a smaller lizard, then a fish, then an invertebrate, then algae, and finally . . . slime.

Splat! The slime splattered into the street and was run over by a car.

All around Koopa Square a cheer went up. Goombas began to dance even more wildly with joy. Mario, Daisy, and Luigi hugged each other. Suddenly someone gasped, 'The fungus!'

Mario and the others looked around.

'It's disappearing!' Luigi shouted.

All over the square the fungus receded, pulling itself backwards, disappearing into cracks. *Splash.* The dried-out, fungus-clogged water fountain gushed to life. Luigi closed his hand around Daisy's.

'Come on,' he said. 'Let's go home.'

But Daisy stopped him.

115

'I . . . I can't,' she stammered, pulling her hand back.

'What do you mean?' Luigi asked, astonished.

'I can't go back yet,' Daisy said.

Luigi turned towards her and gazed intensely into her eyes. 'But, Daisy, you know how I feel about you,' he said. 'Even if I don't really know how to say it exactly right. I mean, I want to be with you.'

'You've got to go home,' Daisy said as tears welled up in her eyes. 'And I . . . I have to . . .'

'Look, what she's saying is she loves you,' Mario said impatiently. 'But she's gotta stay here until she really knows where she belongs. And if you love her, you'll understand and you'll leave now before your brother strangles you.'

Mario walked away. Luigi stared back at Daisy, asking with his eyes if his brother was right. Daisy nodded silently. Luigi felt his heart begin to crack as he took Daisy into his arms and kissed her for what might be the very last time.

15

Two weeks later, Mario, Daniella, and Luigi sat in the Marios' apartment, watching themselves on *Our Miraculous World*.

'They returned the missing Brooklyn women,' the announcer was saying, 'and saved a parallel world from a ruthless dictator. I'd call them the Super Mario Brothers. Next on *Our Miraculous World* – The man on the moon is actually Elvis!'

'I guess we gotta watch,' Mario said.

Mario and Daniella clasped hands and smiled at each other. Beside them, Luigi leaned his chin on his hand and moped. It had been a rough two weeks without the woman he loved.

Suddenly they heard a pounding on the door. Before the brothers could get up to answer it, the door flew open, and Daisy stumbled in. Her shirt was scorched and in tatters, her hair tousled, and a fireball gun hung by her side.

'Daisy!' Luigi jumped up and hugged her.

'Luigi!' Daisy quickly kissed him. 'You guys have to come with me! You've got to help me!'

'What?' Luigi asked. 'What's wrong?'

'You're not going to believe it!' Daisy gasped.

'Oh, I'll believe it,' Mario cried, grabbing his tool belt. 'Whatever it is, I'll believe it!'

About the Author

Todd Strasser has written many award-winning novels for young and teenage readers, including *The Accident* and *Friends Till the End*. He is a frequent speaker at middle schools, junior highs, and conferences in the USA. He likes to fish, play tennis, and spend time with his wife and two children. He and Mario recently visited Dinosaur Land, but they never made it out of the Forest of Illusion.

STAY SONIC
THE OFFICIAL SEGA HANDBOOK
Mike Pattenden

He travels at the speed of sound. He is blue. His sneakers are red. He is Sonic the Hedgehog.

But what else do you know? Sonic hasn't always been blue and Robotnik used to be called Dr Kintobor? There was a time when Mobius, Sonic's planet was peaceful, but then Robotnik went beserko – and the rest is history.

So if you want the scam on Sonic, Robotnik, the Badniks and all the rest – hang around. Plus there are exclusive walk-throughs on Sonic II Master System and Megadrive, so you can take on Robotnik and get those chaos emeralds.

It's here. Now. Everything you wanted to know about Sonic, but you did not know who to ask.

SONIC THE HEDGEHOG ADVENTURE
GAMEBOOK 1: ROBOTROPOLIS
James Wallis

Mobius is under threat from the deranged Robotnik. The demented inventor is busy on a master plan building mega-robots. Only you and Sonic can stop him.

Using your skill, speed and agility, you can help Sonic save the day. But think fast and move quickly, Sonic doesn't hang about and there's no time to waste. The future of Mobius depends on you!

SONIC THE HEDGEHOG ADVENTURE
GAMEBOOK 2: THE ZONE RANGERS
James Wallis

Robotnik is turning all the zones into a living nightmare of pollution and destruction. His Mobius mega trash Plan can only be stopped by Sonic, Tails and you!

You have to use all your speed, skill and quick wits to help Sonic save the day. But time is of the essence, as Mobius is decaying with every second. Are you ready for the challenge?

THE JAMES BOND JUNIOR SERIES
by John Vincent

There's never been a spy like 007 – until now! When James Bond Junior sets out to fight crime, the bad guys had better watch out.

LIVE AND LET'S DANCE

James Bond Junior is in a deadly race against the clock! The notorious arms dealer Baron von Skarin plans to assassinate the heir to the throne of Zamora. It's up to James to sneak out of school – to Switzerland – to save the young prince.

Can James survive the attentions of a killer guard dog, dodge heat-seeking missiles, escape from an avalanche, save the prince and get back to Warfield Academy before the headmaster discovers he's missing?

THE EIFFEL TARGET

Now James Bond Jr is *really* angry.

The foul Dr Derange and his creepy partner Skullcap have planted a nuclear bomb in the Eiffel Tower! Their goal: to start a world war and bring about global chaos!

Things are so desperate, the Warfield Academy class trip to Paris has been cancelled. Can James sneak over to France and disarm the warhead? The class trip – and world peace – depend on it . . .

A VIEW TO A THRILL

James Bond Jr's daring last-minute arrival at Warfield Academy gets him into big trouble, even though his classmates are impressed. After all, not everyone arrives in a high-tech car-plane!

What James doesn't know is that the car has a top-secret device hidden inside. Worse, the evil Scumlord, head of S.C.U.M., and his savage henchman Jaws are scheming to steal it – and kidnap James!

Can James escape and foil Scumlord's plan? More importantly, can James get back to school before lights out?

SWEET DREAMS
Kate Daniel

Jan is terrified to go to sleep. Every night in her dreams she relives the blaze that killed her parents. As her dreams grow more vivid, Jan begins to suspect that the fire wasn't an accident: someone murdered her parents, and she thinks she knows who.

Then Jan starts to walk in her sleep, finding herself mysteriously drawn to a series of midnight fires around town. At first the fires are small, but soon one of Jan's classmates – a girl who accused Jan of starting the fires – is horribly disfigured in the flames that destroy her home.

Is Jan's nightmare coming true? Is she an arsonist – and a killer too?

BABYSITTER'S NIGHTMARE
Kate Daniel

Alice Fleming is trapped in a nightmare. Someone's been breaking into houses all over town, stealing and wrecking furniture. The victims all had one thing in common. Alice babysat their kids. The police are ready to lock Alice up, and even her friends are wondering if Alice has a dark side they never knew.

Then one night Alice cancels a babysitting job, and the substitute sitter is murdered. Alice is desperate to find the real killer. But as she follows the killer's trail, is she walking into a deadly trap set just for her?

ACCIDENTS WILL HAPPEN
Kate Daniel

When a film crew arrives to shoot a movie on her parents' ranch, Samantha Phillips expects it to be great. What she doesn't expect, however, is that it may not only change her life – but may *end* it.

As soon as filming begins, a string of accidents plagues the crew. Then one of the 'accidents' kills a young actor. Tim Rafferty, the movie's star and Samantha's new boyfriend, says he suspects someone is really after *him*. But Samantha wonders . . . Tim seems to love the publicity, and she's beginning to think he may be behind it all.

Samantha starts asking questions, and finds out that Tim *always* gets involved with local girls on his films. And one of those girls is dead!

ROBIN HOOD PRINCE OF THIEVES
Simon Green

The legend lives on. Like a flaming arrow, Robin of Locksley emerges from the shadows of Sherwood Forest to blaze a path for the poor and downtrodden. With a mighty band of fighting men by his side – Friar Tuck, Will Scarlet, the noble Saracen called Azeem, and others – Robin wages a magnificent war against the vicious Sheriff of Nottingham . . . and an equally passionate campaign for the heart of the beautiful Maid Marian. Wielding his bow and arrow with deadly accuracy, Robin of Locksley transforms himself into a new kind of hero.

THE ADDAMS FAMILY
Elizabeth Faucher

You haven't lived unless you've met the Addams Family! There's Morticia, the loving, caring mother, Gomez, the devoted but manic father, and their children Pugsley and Wednesday. Pugsley collects road signs, and Wednesday's favourite toy is a headless doll. Then, of course, there's Thing, the Addams Family's pet hand, who is always willing to lend one, when two just aren't enough. With the return of Uncle Fester, the long-lost brother of Gomez, after twenty-five years' absence, the family is complete once again. However, he may look like Uncle Fester, he may even sound like him, but can he really be the missing uncle?